With her window closed against the cold morning air, she couldn't hear what they were saying. But from all appearances, Hank was doing most of the talking. No doubt giving the man the legal help he was seeking. As she watched him smile and gesture with his hands, she saw not the stable, dependable, professional man he had become, but the handsome boy with whom she'd grown up. The boy she'd loved all her life. The boy she still loved. But it was too late. Even if Hank could ever feel the same way about her as she felt about him, it was too late. Much, much too late.

JOYCE LIVINGSTON has done many things in her life (in addition to being a wife, mother of six, and grandmother to oodles of grandkids, all of whom she loves dearly), from being a television broadcaster for eighteen years, to lecturing and teaching on quilting and sewing, to writing magazine articles on a variety of subjects. She's danced with Lawrence Welk, ice-skated with a chimpanzee, had bottles broken over her head by stuntmen, interviewed hundreds of celebrities and controversial figures, and done many other interesting and unusual things. But now, when she isn't off traveling to wonderful and exotic places as a part-time tour escort, her days are spent sitting in front of her computer, creating stories. She feels her writing is a ministry and a calling from God, and she hopes **Heartsong Presents** readers will be touched and uplifted by what she writes. Joyce loves to hear from her readers and invites you to visit her on the Internet at: www.joycelivingston.com.

Books by Joyce Livingston

Be My Valentine

Joyce Livingston

Heartsong Presents

To Matthew, Mark, Luke, and Don Jr. Livingston. Four of the most wonderful, caring, loving sons a mother could ask for (not to mention handsome, witty well, you get the idea). These boys are model husbands who treat their wives with love, honor, and respect, and they are as romantic as their father. When I look for qualities for the heroes in my books, I look to these four men for inspiration, as well as my husband, Don.

With boundless love, Mom

A note from the author:
I love to hear from my readers! You may correspond with me by writing:

Joyce Livingston
Author Relations
PO Box 719
Uhrichsville, OH 44683

ISBN 1-58660-683-2

BE MY VALENTINE

one

"Which nightgown would you prefer, Sir?" The clerk held up a lacy, low-cut, ultra-sheer number in a slinky vibrant red. "One something like this, perhaps? Most women love this gown."

Hank Gordon couldn't remember a time in his life when he'd been more embarrassed. In all the years he and Sheila were married, not one time had he ever been in the women's lingerie section of Beck's Department Store. "Ah—no, nothing like that. You don't understand." He swallowed hard, sure his face was as red as the gown. "Actually, what I wanted was the same gown I'm returning, but in a smaller size."

The shake of her head and the shrug of the woman's narrow shoulders said it all. "I'm sorry, Sir, but we sold out of that particular gown weeks ago. It was a very popular model. Are you sure your wife wouldn't like something a little more—"

Hank's eyes widened. "Oh, it's not for my wife—"

The sales clerk raised a brow. "Well, then, your girlfriend would probably—"

"I don't have a girlfriend," he inserted quickly, though why he owed her an explanation was beyond him. It wasn't exactly the kind of thing you'd discuss with a stranger.

"Look, my friend asked—I—he—" He frowned and sucked in a deep breath before continuing. *This woman must think I'm a total loony.* "It's this way. My best friend bought this gown for his wife." He opened the bag, pulling out the lacy, shimmering nightgown. He was embarrassed just touching it. "It was way too large and, since they were called out of town, he asked me to return it and exchange it for a smaller size."

"I'd definitely take the slinky red one. Your wife will love it!" a pleasant female voice called out from somewhere behind the pair. "Hi, Hank."

5

Hank spun around, a big smile replacing the frown. "Tink! I'd recognize that chirpy voice of yours anywhere. What are you doing back in Juneau?"

Tina Taylor stood on tiptoe and kissed the big man's crimson cheek. "Long story. If you've got time, after you decide which gown to buy for your wife, I'll treat you to a cup of coffee, and we can catch up on old times. I'd heard you got married. Maybe she'd like to join us. I'd love to meet her."

The broad smile vanished as he drew his breath in sharply. "Sheila died, Tink. Nearly eight years ago."

Hank felt her fingers touch his arm, as her sorrow for him spelled out on her face. "Oh, Hank, I feel terrible. I didn't know."

The clerk took the gown from his hand and cleared her throat noisily. "Sorry to interrupt, but I have other customers who need my attention. Have you made your decision yet?"

"Ah—actually, no, I haven't." Hank fished around in his jacket pocket and pulled out a slip of paper. "But I have the sales receipt. Why don't you just credit my friend's charge account, and he can pick out something later, after he gets back in town."

The woman nodded, took the receipt, and headed for the checkout counter.

"Well, do you have time for coffee, or is that lawyer business of yours demanding all your time?" Tina gave his arm a playful pinch. "You are still playing attorney, aren't you?"

Grateful for the change of subject, Hank nodded. The middle of the lingerie sales floor was not exactly the most conducive place to discuss the details of the death of your beloved wife. He was sure Tina sensed that and had come to his rescue. "Yep, sure am, but by your big city standards, I'd say my routine business is pretty boring. How come you're back in Juneau?" He held up a palm between them. "Wait. Don't answer." He signed the refund slip, then grabbed Tina's arm and headed for the elevator. "Let's get out of here. I feel like a voyeur among all these scantily clad mannequins."

The two old friends decided on a small nearby café, walking the short distance in the cold, brisk air, their arms linked.

Hank smiled down at her as he gave her arm a squeeze. "Did your husband come with you?" She had gloves on, but he couldn't remember seeing a wedding ring on her finger at the department store.

Tina Taylor shivered and yanked up the zipper tab on her jacket, pulling it to the top. "Husband? Not yet." A heavy frown momentarily creased her brow. "How about you? Have you remarried since Sheila—" Her unfinished sentence hung heavily in the brisk Alaskan air.

He smiled as visions of Glorianna, the woman he'd nearly married two years after his wife's death, flooded his mind. "Nearly did, once. But it didn't work out."

"Brrr, I'd forgotten how cool it can get in Juneau this time of year." Tina shivered and pulled the collar up about her neck.

Once again, Hank was sure Tina had changed the subject to spare him the misery of having to talk about something that was obviously painful to him. Her renewed smile pulled his thoughts away. The woman still seemed to have a sixth sense. Her melodious laughter brought back joyful memories long forgotten.

"Do you remember when Mr. Halston gave us flashlights for Christmas? I think we were eight years old. We sat on your mom's steps shining their beams at the passing cars?"

"We sure thought we were doing something naughty, didn't we, Tink?" He slipped his arm about her waist and ushered her through the door of the little café fronting Gastineau Bay. "We had some great times growing up."

"I always wished my mother could be like yours."

"My mom loved you, Tink."

She grinned over her shoulder as they made their way to an empty table in a far corner. "You're the only one who ever called me Tink." With a melancholy sigh, she unzipped her jacket and pulled it from her shoulders. "I've missed being called by that name."

Hank took it from her and pulled out a chair, motioning her to be seated. "Well, you'll always be my Tinker Bell." Once she was settled, he slipped off his stylish black cashmere overcoat and placed both garments on an empty chair. "Remember how my mom would read Peter Pan to us when we'd been good? We both loved that story."

"And we made paper wings for me to wear and a green paper hat and cape for you."

"And a wand from a stick and a Ping-Pong ball. Tinker Bell and Peter Pan. What imaginations we had back then." Hank handed her a menu and began to peruse his own. "We made our own fun, didn't we?"

"We were quite a pair, weren't we?" Tina asked, laughing, still holding the unopened menu.

"That we were." Hank closed his menu and leaned across the table, taking Tina's hand in his. "Remember when we rigged that rope from the rafters in the barn and swung from it, playing like Wendy was there with us? It's a wonder one of us didn't break an arm."

She giggled, her free hand cupping his. "Or a leg! We were pretty daring, as I recall. Especially you!"

"We were more than daring. More like stupid! But what fun we had."

"Oh, Hank, you were always my very best friend. I loved those days."

"Me too. We were really a couple of dreamers, you and me, with big plans for our futures. We were going to have it all."

"Yes, we certainly were dreamers." A heavy sigh emitted from deep within her chest as her smile disappeared, and she gazed into his eyes. "Sometimes I wonder if I should've stayed in Juneau, instead of going off to make my fortune in the big city. Things were always so peaceful here. Maybe if—"

Her sudden change of attitude gave Hank cause for concern. "So? Did you?"

The wistful look disappeared, and she gave him a blank stare. "Did I what?"

"Make your fortune in the big city. Chicago? Isn't that where you went?"

"A fortune? Hardly!" She grimaced as she pulled her hands from his. "Even after all these years, all I have to show for my time and effort is a partially paid-for condo, a broken-down car, and a bunch of monthly bills. Living in the big city is not cheap, and my life didn't exactly pan out the way I'd planned. Things happen"—she snapped her fingers—"and your life changes in an instant."

The waitress brought two large coffee mugs to their table and filled them to the brim without asking, placing two packets of creamer beside Hank's cup.

Tina covered her cup with her palm and shook her head.

"You ready to order, or you need a little more time?"

With a wave of his hand toward the waitress, Hank picked up his menu again. "Give us a few more minutes."

They sat silently as the woman gave them an impatient nod and moved on.

"So what're you doing back in town? Juneau's a long way from Chicago. Or anywhere," he added, forcing a big grin, Tina's comment still niggling at his mind.

She stretched first one arm, then the other, as she settled back in her chair and folded her hands in her lap. "Tell me about it! If I sound a bit flaky it's because my body is still on Chicago time. I may have trouble adjusting to Alaska's long, dark winter days. It's never dark in Chicago. Not with all the lights and all the activity going on twenty-four-seven. And it's never quiet. Cars, trains, planes, the El. But you adjust. I guess I'll adjust here too, but it may take me awhile. I'll probably have to sleep with the lights on and a radio blaring." She raised her brows. "But then, there's the flip side. Those wonderful long, lazy summer days filled with sunshine!"

He brightened. "You make it sound like you'll be staying for awhile."

She picked up her cup and blew into it, eyeing him over the rim. "Looks like I'm here to stay."

"Permanently?" He stared at his old friend. Although she was smiling, he detected a note of sadness in her tone.

"Umm, not exactly permanently."

"You two ready to order?"

The pair had been so engrossed in their conversation, they hadn't noticed the waitress standing beside them again, with her pad and pencil in hand.

Hank nodded toward Tina. "The soup and sandwich special okay with you? It's usually pretty good."

"Fine."

Hank took their menus and stuffed them into the little holder mounted on the wall before turning his attention back to his guest. "Okay, tell me what you meant by that comment about being here permanently, for awhile. Somehow those two terms don't jibe."

A sadness covered her face as she lowered her eyes, her fingers methodically tracing the edge of the cup. "It's my grandmother. She's not at all well."

"Oh no. I'm so sorry to hear that, Tink. I remember how much you loved her."

Her lips began to quiver and she blinked hard. "She's dying, Hank."

"Harriett Taylor is dying? I don't understand. If she's dying and she's in Chicago, what are you doing back here in Juneau? Knowing you, and how close you two were, I'm surprised you didn't want to stay there with her."

He watched as Tina blinked and rubbed at her eyes, as if to fight back tears. He knew firsthand how important her grandmother had always been to her. He well remembered how her mother had abandoned her less than six months after her father had committed suicide and taken off with one of her surly boyfriends, who didn't want a teenage girl tagging along. Although Hank had only been a junior in high school at the time, he'd wanted to hunt the woman down, make her come back, and face up to her responsibility.

"We—we're both moving back here. The doctor said it's

only a matter of time for Gram. After that—" She paused. "I guess I'll be heading back to Chicago."

The pitiful look on Tina's face made him want to pull her into his arms and comfort her, but he sat quietly and listened, offering her his handkerchief instead.

She dabbed at her eyes before going on. "She's never complained, but I know she's hated living at the care home. It's depressing. I wanted to keep her with me, but with working, commuting, and being away so many hours each day, it was impossible. She's been so good to me. I've felt awful about her living there, but we had no other choice."

"I'm sure she understood." Hank's hand again cupped hers across the table. "She knew you had obligations."

"I–I hope so. I've tried to spend as much time with her as I could, but I'm afraid it hasn't been enough."

"You had your own life to live."

She lowered her gaze and dabbed with the handkerchief again. "I–I know. I've tried to tell myself that same thing. For the first few years, I rushed home from the office each day to be with her. But then, I guess I coaxed myself into believing I had my rights too. I–I've left her alone way more than I should have. Now—"

"Surely she's made friends at the care home."

"She has, but I know it isn't the same as having family with you. Many of the ladies who room around her are much worse off than she is. It's heartbreaking. Some are like—I hate to say it—like vegetables. The lights are on, but there's no one at home. It's been hard on her. Unlike them, her mind is as sharp as ever. It's her body that's giving out."

"She's getting old, Tink. That's what happens. It's inevitable. It'll get us too, eventually."

The two sat silently sipping their coffee, watching as the waitress brought their orders.

"You didn't explain about moving back here," Hank pressed easily once the woman had moved on. From the weary look on Tina's face it was obvious the whole situation was stressing her out.

She picked up her spoon and stirred at the steaming soup in her bowl. "I work for a huge parts company and have since the first year I moved to Chicago. They ship parts all over the world."

He ripped open a bag of oyster crackers and dumped them into his bowl. "Even Juneau?"

A faint smile curled up the corners of her mouth. "Even Juneau. Times have changed, Hank, and unlike some companies, my company has changed with those times. We were one of the first major corporations to move our enormous catalog onto the Web. It nearly doubled our business that first year. I was one of the ones who got the catalog up and running. Because of it, and the whopping increase in sales, I got a nice promotion."

Hank did an exaggerated applause. "Good for you! I'm sure you deserved it."

"Not long ago, I was promoted to senior design technologist and became part of the distribution management team. Most of my work now is done independently, using the Internet. Makes me pretty much a loner, but I like it."

"Well, belated congratulations. I hope your promotion meant more money!"

She nodded and took a bite of her sandwich before going on. "It did, but it also means a bit of traveling too, when our team gets together face to face. I've only had to leave Gram maybe two or three times so far, but I'm always worried I'll be in Dallas or New Orleans or some other faraway place when she really needs me. Especially now."

Hank motioned for the waitress to refill their cups, then picked up his sandwich, waving it toward her. "Tink, that still doesn't explain why you're back in Juneau. Now I'm really confused."

With a slight grin she held up a hand between them. "Patience, Peter Pan. I'm coming to that. When the doctor told me he didn't think Gram would last another year, I knew

I had to find some way to spend more time with her."

"That sounds like you."

"I had to get her out of that care home. All she's talked about, since she's taken a turn for the worse, is how much she'd like to come back home to die. Back to Juneau."

Hanks brows rose quickly. "You're bringing her here?"

"Yes, she's already here! I called ahead, and they had a vacancy in a nice facility not far from her house. I took her there as soon as we got off the plane. I'll move her into her home as soon as I can get it ready. I knew she'd never be able to take the dust and the noise while I'm cleaning up her place and doing a bit of remodeling. Not to mention the paint fumes. Right now her place is a pretty big mess."

"Sounds like you have your work cut out for you. I guess you'll be looking for a job after that."

"No, I convinced my boss I can work from here. The majority of what I do is on the computer and the Internet anyway, so it won't make any difference where I'm located."

"That's great!" Hank frowned. "I didn't know she still owned that old house. I figured it'd been sold years ago."

"No, she still owns it. She's kept the taxes paid on it. I tried to talk her into renting it out, but she wouldn't hear of it. She's had herself convinced from the time we left that someday she'd come back to it."

"Now she's here."

Tina nodded. "Yes, she's here."

"Thanks to you."

"It's the least I could do for her."

Hank finished off his sandwich and took a final sip of coffee. He hated to bring it up, but the question plagued him. He'd driven by the old house several months earlier and hoped Tina's expectations weren't set too high. "Have you seen her house lately? It's looking kind of shabby."

"I know. After I got Gram settled, I had the taxi driver drive me past. You're right. It is in pretty bad shape, at least the roof is, and it needs painting and a general cleanup. But it seems structurally sound. I'm sure the inside needs remodeling from top to bottom. But Gram thinks she has enough money to do it, and she's thrilled with the idea. You're probably wondering why she'd want to go to all the trouble and expense of fixing up her home when she has so little time."

"It had entered my mind."

"Not only is it filled with precious memories for her, she's never liked the idea of me living in Chicago. Particularly after she's gone."

He watched as she blinked a few times.

"She's always said Juneau is a much better and safer place for a single woman to live. Gram is hoping, once the house is fixed up, I'll stay on and live in it. After she—" She paused, as if the words stuck in her throat. "I've taken a temporary leave to get the place ready."

Figuring it'd probably be best to not pursue that subject, seeing how much even the thought of losing her grandmother upset her, he asked, "What about your condo?"

She shrugged and let out a sigh. "I've sublet it."

"Sounds like you've thought of everything." He wiped at his mouth, then placed his napkin on the table. "By the way, where are you staying until you get the house fixed up?"

She crossed her arms over her chest as she stared into the half-eaten bowl of cold soup. "I stayed at a motel last night. I'd hoped I could stay at Gram's house, but until I can get a plumbing and heating man to check out that old furnace and see if the hot water tank needs replacing and get someone to reroof the place, I guess I'll still be staying at the motel."

Hank stood, offered his hand, and pulled her up beside him. "Oh no, you won't. You're staying with me. I've got plenty of room."

She backed away and stared at him. "Stay with you? Impossible! How would it look, a reputable man like you moving a strange woman into his house?"

"You're not strange—" Hank paused and gave her a side-ways grin. "Well, not very, anyway. You're an old friend. And besides, I have a housekeeper who lives there full-time. It'll be perfectly proper." He picked up her coat and held it open for her as she slipped into it with a smile that warmed his heart.

"The motel is fine, Hank. Honest. I can't ask you to go out of your way for me."

He put on his overcoat, picked up the ticket, looked it over, and left several dollar bills on the table. "Look, Tink. I've been rattling around in that big old house of mine for more years than I care to count. I'd welcome the company. Maybe I can even offer you a helping hand. I swing a pretty mean hammer and could sure use the exercise."

She gave him an incredulous look. "You're serious!"

"Serious as a dog with a bone. Tell me the name of your motel, give me a few more hours at the office, and I'll pick you up and take you to my place. I'll even call Faynola and tell her to put on a pot of spaghetti." He gave her a friendly wink as his hand went to the small of her back and he ushered her toward the cashier. "As I recall, spaghetti is your favorite dish."

"Faynola? Who's Faynola?"

"My housekeeper." He handed the cashier the ticket and his credit card, signed his name, and in seconds they were on their way out the door. "Faynola's getting pretty old, but she's still a great cook and a terrific housekeeper. You've got to promise not to tell any of my friends, or they'll try to hire her out from under me. I keep her talents a big secret."

"I'm amazed that you remembered my spaghetti fetish. Even after all these years, it's still my favorite."

Hank wrapped his coat about him to ward off the chilling winds coming off the Bay. "Of course I remember, Tink. And I'll have her chop some fresh onion and grate plenty of parmesan cheese. As I recall, that's the way you like it."

"You're still the same old sweetie." She reached her gloved hand up and cupped his cheek. "My very own Peter Pan."

two

"Hank, this really isn't necessary, you know. The motel was fine." Tina took her small suitcase from his hand and placed it on the bed.

He pressed a finger to her lips. "Enough. Not another word. This is your home, until you're ready to move into your grandmother's house. You hear me?"

She took a couple of bounces on the bed, testing its softness, and smiled up at him. "Peter Pan, ever to my rescue."

"Hey, stop. You're making me blush."

"I appreciate your invitation, but fixing Gram's house is going to take awhile, and I'll want to spend some time with her each day. I can't impose upon you for that long. If you'll let me stay for a week or two, at least until I get my bearings, I'll either move into Gram's house or find another place to stay."

"My answer to you about finding another place is an emphatic no, but if it will make you happy, we'll worry about that later. Right now you need to get settled in here."

"Thank you, Hank."

"You're welcome. Mi casa es su casa."

"Wow! Who is that?" Tina asked as a beautiful Siberian husky came bounding into the room.

Hank leaned over and stroked the dog's head. "Hey, Ryan, Old Boy, I wondered where you were."

"Ryan? What a great name." She scooted off the bed and moved cautiously toward the pair. "Can I pet him?"

Hank grinned. "Sure."

She ran a hand over the dog's soft fur, then patted him on the head. "You're a real beauty."

"The two of us took second in the annual Sourdough Dogsled Nightshirt Race a couple of years ago. He's a born

16

leader. I really should give him to someone who races dogs on a regular basis, but I couldn't bear to part with him. He's a great companion." He let loose a slight chuckle. "But a poor substitute for a good wife."

Tina stared into his kind face as she continued to pat the dog. "Hank, how did you know Sheila was the one for you? I mean—how can you tell when you're in love? Truly in love."

He appeared thoughtful. "Boy, you're asking a tough question. Well," he began slowly, his gaze drifting to the picture of his deceased wife on the dresser, "I can't say lightning bolts split the sky or rainbows appeared in the north, but—I knew. The moment I held her in my arms that very first time, I knew we were destined to be together. It was a feeling—no, not just a feeling—an assurance deep in my gut—I was hers, and she was mine. No rockets went off, no blaring horns, no shooting stars, but I knew. Sounds crazy, doesn't it? I think God puts that special feeling in your heart when you've met the one He has planned for you, and you just know. That's the best way I can explain it. Sorry I'm not more eloquent."

"But—what if you're not sure you're feeling that special feeling? I mean, do you think you can learn to love someone?"

He let out a long, slow gush of air. "Now that one is a toughie. In Bible times marriages were arranged, and I guess those people learned to love one another. That, or they accepted their fate and learned to live with it."

"Could you? Learn to love someone?"

"Umm, no. I don't think so. I'm kind of a romantic guy at heart. I believe in the romantic kind of love between a man and a woman. Why?"

Tina bit at her lip and avoided Hank's eyes. "Just curious."

"How about you? Do you think you could learn to love someone who couldn't sweep you off your feet with his smile? Or his touch?"

"I'd like to think I could learn to love him. In time. If there were reason enough."

He frowned. "Reason enough? What reason could there

ever be that would make you marry a guy you didn't love?"

"This is a beautiful room," she commented casually, looking around for the first time, hoping he wouldn't pursue his question. "I'll bet your wife decorated it."

Hank's expression became even more somber as he, too, looked around the meticulously decorated room. "She did. Right after Sheila learned she had cancer, she was like a wild woman. Everything she'd ever wanted to do she tried to crowd into those last few months before the weakness set in. Redecorating this room was one of the projects she'd had on her to-do list for several years and had never gotten around to it. This room was one of the guest rooms, but it ended up being her room when we had to bring in the hospital bed. She couldn't manage the steps up to our bedroom." He turned away, and she almost wished she hadn't mentioned Sheila's name.

"Go, Ryan," he said pointing toward the door. "I'll bet Faynola has a treat for you in the kitchen."

Tina's heart went out to Hank as the two of them watched the big dog obey his master and saunter out of the room. What an ordeal he'd been through. Losing a loved one to death had to be one of life's most difficult, hard-to-bear experiences. Now that she was about to lose her grandmother, the person she loved more than anyone else in the world, she could only imagine the pain and suffering she'd be facing in the not-so-distant future. She stood up beside him and kissed his cheek. "I'm sorry. I know how much you must have loved her."

Blinking, Hank took her hand in his and stared into her eyes. "I always held onto that tenuous thread of hope, praying constantly, but God must have had other plans. He didn't answer."

"Gram says God always answers our prayers. Just not always the way we want them answered or when we want them answered. But it's sure hard to understand why he'd take Sheila away from you. Were you—" Her voice trailed off.

Hank backed away a bit, but still held onto her hand. "Was I what? Angry?"

She nodded.

"At first I was. I even tried to bargain with God. I actually threatened Him, telling Him if He took her I'd know He wasn't real, and if He wasn't real, there was no reason I'd ever pray to Him again. But after awhile I got over it and realized I was being childish."

"I'm having a hard time dealing with Gram leaving me, and she's old. I can't imagine losing someone as young and vital as Sheila. She had so much to live for."

Hank let loose of her hand, turning his back to her. "We both wanted children, Tink. We thought she was pregnant. That's when we found out about her cancer. When we went for the pregnancy test."

"Was she?" Tina asked, keeping her voice barely audible.

He nodded. "Yes. One of the happiest days of our lives turned out to be the saddest."

Tina stepped forward, looped her arms about his waist, and pressed her face against his back. "The baby?"

"He didn't make it. He never had a chance. She miscarried in her second trimester." Tina could feel the sobs wracking at his body as she pulled him close. "I not only lost my wife, I lost my son."

"I–I wish I'd known her."

"You would've loved her, Tink. Everyone did. We had some wonderful times together those last few months. Times I'll never forget."

"I guess you can be thankful for that much. At least she wasn't taken from you suddenly." She wished she had the proper words to console him, but somehow they didn't come.

"I know. I told myself that a hundred times, but it didn't lessen the pain when the final day came."

"I'm sorry about the baby. You'd have made a terrific daddy."

"I sure would've tried. I wanted to be as good a dad to my son as my dad had been to me."

"Your dad was the best. I used to look at him and fantasize that he was my father. I'd have given anything to have had your dad for a father, instead of the poor excuse of a man my mother married. Of course, she wasn't much better than he was."

Hank pulled away from her grasp, turned, and wrapped his arms about her, pulling her close. "I can't tell you how many times I wanted to go to your house and kick your father's shins. Seems funny now that I'm a grown man, but as a young boy, that was the worst thing I could think of to do to him. I never figured out exactly what I would do to your mom, but I hated the way she neglected you."

Tina let out a slight giggle. "Kick him in the shins, eh?"

"Uh-huh. And I had a second plan."

"Oh? What?"

"Promise you won't laugh, if I tell you?"

"I promise."

"I–I planned to get you to run away with me, and I was going to marry you and take care of you. I think I was about eight at the time. Your dad had just given you a hard whipping for knocking over his can of beer."

"You actually thought of marrying me when you were eight years old? You never told me."

He grinned sheepishly. "I know. It was one of my boyish dreams. I wanted to be your hero. But I figured you'd say no, so I kept my mouth shut."

She tapped the tip of his nose with her fingertip. "You should've asked me. I might've said yes. But then both our lives would've been different. You wouldn't have married Sheila, and I wouldn't be—"

He harrumphed, apparently not even realizing she'd quit talking midsentence. "I'm not sure they would've given a marriage license to a couple of eight year olds. You were my very best friend. I wanted to protect you."

"I knew that, Hank. You were always there for me. And believe me, it helped."

"And I'm here for you now." He backed away and pointed to the huge suitcase standing in the middle of the floor. "Now unpack. Faynola will have dinner on the table at seven." He spun around on his heels and headed for the door. "I'm going back to the office for a couple of hours to catch up on a few things. If you need anything tell Faynola."

Tina watched as he shut the door behind him. Hank may have thought their relationship had been platonic, but that's not the way she'd seen it. She'd loved him from the time they were children right on up through high school, but she'd never felt worthy of him. Hank had been the brainy one, always excelling in academics. The athletic one, the football captain, the point guard, the distance runner, lettering in all the sports. The popular one, the one the girls all wanted to date, and the guys looked up to. What had she been? An uninteresting girl with mediocre grades, from a dysfunctional family who lived constantly in poverty, with a job after school that made it impossible for her to go out for sports. Although she'd had many friends, she was never elected prom queen or to any class office. She'd been the one sitting on the sidelines, cheering loudly, while Hank had been the center of attention. But Hank, dear, sweet, lovable Hank, had never turned his back on her, no matter how popular he'd been. She'd always remained his best friend, and she'd never told him how much she loved him, for fear it would end their relationship.

Slowly, she dropped down on the bed, kicked off her shoes, and picked up the phone, dialing the number from memory.

A sleepy male voice answered on the fifth ring.

"Hi. It's me. I'm in Juneau. But my plans have changed."

❧

Tina unpacked, putting her things in the guest room's empty drawers and hanging her clothing in the spacious closet. It was a beautiful room, the kind of room she'd always dreamed of having one day. It was burgundy, green, and white, with a very feminine rose motif and thick, plush burgundy wall-to-wall carpeting. She wondered about the woman who had so painstakingly decorated it and tried to visualize the room with a hospital bed, instead of the magnificent rice bed that now stood in its place.

After a leisurely shower, she dressed in a soft slip-on sweater and jeans and pulled her shoulder-length brown hair up in a ponytail. It was still only five. She accepted a cup of steaming hot tea from Faynola and wandered into the den, pleased to find several bookcases. After letting her finger trail across the titles of at least fifty books, most of them on law, she located one shelf that harbored books on art and interior decorating. She selected several that dealt with remodeling, took them back to her room, and seated herself on the rose-colored chaise lounge in front of the big bedroom window that overlooked Gastineau Bay.

At seven straight up, Hank rapped on her door and led her into the cozy kitchen, where the big round table was set for two.

"I didn't hear you drive in."

He grinned. "Faynola said you were reading. You were probably too engrossed in some sappy romance novel."

She elbowed him. "I would've been if I could've found one, but apparently you don't keep a good selection on hand."

Hank pulled out her chair, then seated himself opposite her. "Did you find everything you need? If not—"

Her hand rested on his. "Hey, you don't have to take care of me, you know. I'm a big girl now. I've grown up."

He gazed at her for a moment before answering. "I know. I can see that, and you've turned into quite a woman."

She tilted her head and lifted a brow. "Is that a compliment?"

"You bet."

After Hank thanked the Lord for their food, they devoured delicious dinner salads, topped with the best dill dressing Tina had ever tasted. Hank explained it was made from one of Faynola's secret recipes.

"Here you are. Spaghetti, just like you requested, Mr. Gordon." Faynola placed the steaming platter of spaghetti and meatballs in the center of the table. "I've chopped plenty of onion and grated the Parmesan, just like you said."

Tina took in a deep breath. The spaghetti smelled divine.

Usually she prepared the meatless kind in the tiny kitchen of her condo, and it was nothing to brag about. She couldn't remember the last time she'd had spaghetti that looked, or smelled, this good. "It looks wonderful, Faynola. Thank you. I hope you didn't go to a lot of trouble. Hank didn't give you much notice."

Faynola gave her employer an adoring look. "For Mr. Gordon, I'd do anything. He's the nicest man in the world." The older woman beamed at him in a motherly fashion.

Hank shyly ducked his head and blushed as he pointed his finger toward the sink. "Faynola, go, before you give me a big head. Compliments won't get you a raise. I keep telling you, you're overpaid as it is."

Tina grabbed the woman's arm before she could get away. "Don't pay any attention to him, Faynola. I want to hear more about this man. I haven't seen him in years. Surely he isn't the nicest man in the world! He has to have a few flaws. Like leaving his dirty socks on the floor? Or spattering shaving cream on the bathroom mirror?"

With a quick glance toward her smiling employer, Faynola shook her head. "Oh no, Ma'am, he never does anything like that. When I—"

Hank smiled but put up his hand to silence her. "No! Not another word. You've said enough already."

"But I want to hear all—" Tina began.

"No more, ladies. Let's just let this subject drop."

Tina turned the woman loose. "You can tell me when Mr. Grumpy is away, Faynola. Okay?"

The woman grinned, nodded, and backed away toward the sink again. "Yes, Ma'am, enjoy your dinner."

"A terrific dinner and good company, what more could a woman ask?" Tina placed her fork on the plate, took the last nibble of garlic bread, and leaned back in her chair, touching the corners of the napkin to her lips.

Hank folded his own napkin slowly, his eyes never leaving hers. "What more? Let me see if I can take care of that question." He called for Faynola, and she came over with a tray bearing two large crystal dishes, which she placed in front of Tina first, then Hank.

Tina stared at the bowls, then lifted her eyes to meet Hank's. "You remembered. Raspberry sherbet. My favorite."

"I wasn't sure if it's still your fave. It's been a long time."

"Well, it still is." She spooned up a big bite and slowly placed it on her tongue, savoring the robust flavor. "This brings back so many memories. Evenings sitting on your parents' porch, swinging on the porch swing, listening to the radio. Actually, I think it was your mom who got me hooked on this stuff in the first place."

"It was always her favorite too. But be careful, that stuff is cold! It'll go to your head in no time."

"Umm, this is fabulous." She twirled her spoon through the deep pink concoction, all the while keeping her eyes on her host. "Your housekeeper was right. You are a nice man."

"That just goes to show how trusting you are. Actually, I'm an ax murderer."

"Peter Pan? An ax murderer? I hardly think so."

When they finished their meal, Tina insisted on placing their dishes in the dishwasher before allowing Hank to lead her into the living room.

"Sit, Ryan," he told the big dog, who was following at their heels.

Tina smiled as she watched Ryan immediately obey his master. "Good dog."

"I told Faynola to bring our coffee in here." He motioned toward the deep mauve damask sofa, waiting for her to be seated before dropping down beside her.

After Tina took a few sips of her coffee, she took stock of their surroundings. Everything in the room was elegant, from the silk-knotted drapery cords to the lighted, professionally framed artwork on the walls. "What a beautiful room. I assume Sheila did the decorating in here too?"

Hank smiled proudly. "Uh-huh, she did the whole house,

all except the fourth bedroom. She didn't have time to do it before—" He stopped midsentence and gazed toward the window.

"I'm so sorry, Hank. I wish there was something I could do to take away the pain."

He let out a long, slow sigh. "It's better now. Honest it is. It's just that I haven't talked with anyone about it for so long—"

"And here I am, asking all sorts of questions."

Tina's heart was touched just thinking about the kind of love Hank must've had for his wife.

"I think seeing you again has brought back all the old memories." Hank gave her wistful smile. "You know, I really have dealt with this loss. A long time ago. Sometimes, though, I still get a little sad."

"Of course you do. It's perfectly understandable that you'd be a little sad from time to time. It sounds as though the two of you had a wonderful marriage."

He nodded. "We did."

"You mentioned you'd nearly married again?"

He leaned back into the sofa and spread his arms wide across the back, crossing his ankles and staring at the ceiling. "Yep, I did. I met this really special woman. Glorianna Kane. She'd lost her husband, who was a real scoundrel by the way, in a tragic accidental shooting."

"Was she from around here?"

"No, but you may remember her aunt Anna. She owned that big quilt shop downtown, across from where the cruise ships dock."

"The Bear Paw? Of course I remember her. Anna was a nice lady. In fact, I worked in her shop one summer as a cashier. She was a terrific employer."

"Well," he went on, "Glorianna is her niece. Anna passed away a few years ago and left everything to her. I handled the legal part of it. She was from Kansas City."

"But you didn't marry her?"

Hank pursed his lips and shook his head. "Nope. My best

friend married her. Took her right out from under my nose at the altar."

Tina's jaw dropped. "You're kidding, right?"

"Nope, Trapper—"

"Not the Trapper Timberwolf we went to school with!"

"Yep. One and the same."

"But he was always such a nice guy. What happened to him?"

Faynola brought in the tray with more coffee. Hank motioned to her to place it on the table, then waited for her to leave the room before continuing. "Trapper was—and still is—a nice guy."

"But surely he's not your best friend anymore!"

"Yep, believe it or not, he is." Hank slapped his knee and laughed aloud. "Actually, I was the best man at their wedding."

"No!" Tina gave him an incredulous stare. "If you were, I'd say you were the best man, in more ways than one."

Hank laughed, as he filled her cup and handed it to her, before filling his own. "The two of them belonged together. I knew it right from the start, but I was too stubborn to admit it. I'm sure now, looking back, I was only kidding myself when I thought Glorianna could forget her love for Trapper and love me." He blew into the steaming hot liquid, his gaze never leaving her face. "You know, losing her nearly killed me, but I loved her enough to want to see her happy. Trapper was the man for her. I finally admitted it, despite my feelings for her."

Tina lifted her own cup in a mock salute. "To you, Hank Gordon. You are truly an amazing man."

His hand went up between them as he shook his head. "Nothing amazing about it. I just came face to face with the facts, was smart enough to accept them, and probably saved all of us a whole bunch of grief. Too many folks find out they've made a mistake after it's too late. I was lucky enough to find out first."

"Do you—"

"Still love her?" He stared off in space, as if asking himself that same question. "Nope, not anymore. I can honestly say I'm over it. Sometimes I wonder if much of what I thought was love for Glorianna was really loneliness. Maybe I was in love with the idea of being in love again. Who knows?"

Tina bristled at the thought of someone treating Hank so callously. "I can't imagine a woman doing something like that to a fine man like you. I'm surprised you'll have anything to do with either of them. Sounds to me like you'd be better off without them."

Hank quickly turned to face her, a frown deeply etched on his forehead. "Don't say that, Tink. She never meant to hurt me. Glorianna is one of the finest women I've ever known."

"Doesn't sound like it to me!" *But who am I to judge?* she asked herself. *With my lousy track record?*

"Well, she is, and I want you to meet her. I'm sure you two'll really hit it off." His face softened. "She's a lot like you."

"Oh?" Tina grimaced. "I'm not sure I'm glad to hear those words."

"It was a compliment, believe me. You'll see, when you meet her. Glorianna is a very special person, and you'll love her kids."

Tina's brows raised. "She and Trapper have children?"

Hank grinned as he pointed to a framed photograph on the mantel. "Oh yes. Todd was seven when she came to Alaska. Then little Emily Anna was born on their wedding night, and—"

"On their wedding night?" Tina leaned back into the sofa, her hand going to her forehead. "What kind of a woman is she anyway? And Trapper? I can't believe he'd get a woman pregnant and then not marry her until time for their baby to be born!"

❧

"Whoa, there. You're judging them too harshly. Let me explain." Hank rose and walked to the fireplace, fetched the photo, and placed it in her hands. "Glorianna's husband died in an accident. Not long after that, she was notified she'd inherited her aunt's quilt shop here in Juneau, and she moved up here. That's when she met Trapper."

"And you?"

"Yes, and she met me. I was her aunt's attorney and took care of all the paperwork for her."

"And you fell in love with her. So how did Trapper get into the picture?"

"Actually, he came into the picture first, way ahead of me, and things were going pretty well for the two of them. But when Glorianna found out she was pregnant, he had a bit of trouble—"

"He had a bit of trouble?" Tina turned her head away and shoved the photo towards Hank. "What a creep!"

"No, you've got it all wrong." Hank shook his head vigorously. "Trapper wasn't the baby's father. Her deceased husband was!"

"Whew, that's a relief. For a minute there I thought old Trapper'd been ready to desert the woman when he found out he was going to be a daddy. This sounds like one of the TV soaps!"

"No, he'd never do anything like that. But the news did come as a shock to him. He took off in that seaplane of his to do some big job up in Fairbanks and was gone for a number of weeks. That's when I came into the picture, as you so delicately put it."

Tina gave him a sideways grin. "So? Who came on to whom?"

Hank flinched. "It wasn't like that, Tink. I went to Glorianna's place as her attorney and ended up fixing a leaky pipe."

"That's a new approach."

"It wasn't meant to be an approach. You might remember the Calhouns. They're clients of mine now, and they'd asked me to dinner. So, knowing Glorianna didn't know many folks in town and hadn't had a chance to get out much since she'd arrived, after I fixed the pipe, I invited her to go with me. She accepted, and we had a lovely evening. So it was only natural that I invite her out again. One thing led to another and, voilà! I was in love!"

"But was she?"

Her question hit him hard right in the heart. Had he only kidded himself into thinking Glorianna had been in love with him? Because he'd so desperately wanted a wife and family? "I–I thought so. I think she honestly thought she loved me too. After all, you said it yourself, I'm a good guy."

"You are, and she'd have been lucky to have married you. I hope Trapper is living up to her expectations. You had to have been a hard act to follow."

Hank lowered himself onto the sofa beside her and took the photo from her hands, staring at each smiling face as he remembered the day that was to have been his wedding day. "Trapper finally came to his senses. He did the only thing he could think of to stop the wedding. He snatched my bride away from me at the altar."

"You're kidding, right? Things like that only happen in romance novels."

"Oh, it happened all right. He burst into the church, grabbed her up in his arms, and took off with her in that souped-up pickup of his. It all happened so fast, everyone just stood there watching. Me included."

"Did you go after her?"

"Yes, once I realized what was happening. But it was too late. In my heart I knew he'd done the right thing. I just didn't want to admit it to anyone."

Tina let out a long breath of air. "Okay, so he captured your bride, but you were kidding me about being the best man at their wedding, weren't you? After what they'd put you through?"

"I was shocked when Trapper asked me. I wanted to deck him."

"Why didn't you? You had every right."

Hank's finger traced the fluted edge of the lovely frame. "I guess God intervened. Somehow, the hurt and embarrassment I'd felt seemed to melt away when Trapper apologized for what he'd done. His intention hadn't been to hurt me. It'd been to claim the woman he loved." Hank shrugged. "I was just in the way. Couldn't be mad at a guy forever for that."

"What about her? She could've stopped him, refused to go with him."

"Oh, she struggled. We all saw her do that. Kicking and hitting at him when he scooped her up. We could still hear her screaming as they drove off."

"But his persuasive charms must've won out. She married him," she said with disgust.

"Persuasive charms? I'm not so sure that was it at all. It was their love, Tink. A love so strong, it compelled them both to go against the world to be together."

Tina leaned into Hank and stared at the picture. "What about the baby? Was it really born on their wedding night?"

Hank grinned. "Yep, she sure was, and that little Emily Anna had to be the prettiest little girl ever born."

She smiled up into his face. "She's adorable."

"Trapper and Glorianna have three kids of their own." He pointed to the handsome young man seated on Trapper's lap. "This is Chip. He's about four now. Emily Anna, of course. Here's Todd, their oldest. And this—" He paused, grinned, and pointed to the baby being held by the attractive woman seated beside Trapper who had to be Glorianna, "is the newest addition."

Tina braced her hand against the sofa and raised herself to Hank's level, planting a kiss on his cheek. "What an old softie you are. You're still the same lovable Hank I knew as a child. I just wish there was some way I could take away the pain you've suffered. First you lost your wife. Then Glorianna. You deserve better, Hank. So much better."

His arm circled her shoulders, and he pulled her close. "I think better just arrived. You're here."

three

Hank inserted the key in the lock the next morning, with a backward look. "You sure you want to fix up this old place?"

Tina let out a giggle and shrugged. "Too late to turn back now. Gram is counting on me. Guess I've got my work cut out for me."

The two grinned at one another as the old door creaked open. "Better let me go in first, in case there're any ghosts milling around in there."

"Or worse yet—bats!" Tina nodded, then followed close at his heels, brushing aside a spider's web with a shudder.

"And things that go bump in the night?"

"Those too! Whew, this place really smells musty." She placed her box of cleaning supplies on a table, moved quickly to the big plate-glass window, and flung open the drapes, setting loose a cloud of dust. "I think I could grow plants in here. There must be a quarter inch of dust accumulation."

Hank blinked and fanned a palm before his face, faking a cough. "If you're going to work in here you'd better wear a dust mask. I've got some in my workshop I can let you have. That stuff is really hard on your lungs."

She grabbed at his arm. "Don't worry about me. I'll be fine, and I promise to wear a mask."

He punched a switch on the wall, and the room was instantly flooded with a garish light from the overhead fixture. "You've already had the power turned on?"

"Actually, it was never off. Gram was afraid the pipes would freeze, so she's been paying the fuel and electric bills."

"Tink, it's been several years since your grandmother was home!"

"I know, but you know Gram. She was determined that, one

day, she'd return. I tried to talk her into selling the place, but you remember how headstrong she could be. She's as stubborn as they come. It was her money, so there wasn't much I could do about it."

Hank followed Tina into the kitchen, watching with interest as she turned on both faucets in the old white porcelain sink and a combination of both water and air rumbled out in spurts. How was she ever going to get the place in shape as quickly as she'd planned? To him, it looked like a monumental job. "Don't tell me she paid the water bills too."

"Yep, good thing too. I needed it to get started with my cleaning." She pulled a faded dish towel from a drawer, dampened it, and began wiping off the countertop, turning the dust to mud. "I went shopping yesterday and bought those cleaning supplies. Oh, and I've had the phone turned on. I didn't want to be here alone without a phone."

While she opened cupboard doors and checked shelves and drawers, Hank turned up the thermostat on the furnace, made sure the refrigerator was running, and checked out the burners and the oven. "Other than being dusty, things seem to be in good shape," he told her, brushing his hands together.

"I'll have to take down the curtains and wash the windows. And the linoleum needs a good coat of wax. And the cabinets need new shelf paper, and I'd like to paint the walls and put up a new border around the ceiling. Maybe some yellow sunflowers. Gram always liked sunflowers. And—"

"Whoa!" Hank spun her around to face him, his hands gently clamping her shoulders. "I thought you were just going to clean the place up, I didn't know you were planning an entire remodeling job."

"It's for Gram, Hank."

Her face took on a serious air, and he was sure she was blinking back tears. He wished he hadn't teased her about her exuberance for the old house.

"She deserves the best, and I'm going to do what I can to make it happen for her."

"And I'm going to help you," he told her, planting a kiss on her forehead before rubbing his hands together expectantly.

"I can't ask you to do that. You've got a law practice to take care of, not to mention your personal life. I'm sure I can hire someone to help me."

"Look, Tink, I try to keep my work load down to eight-to-five weekdays, so I'm available to help you every evening and all weekend. Besides, I could use the exercise. You'll be doing me a big favor if you'll let me help you."

"No, it's asking too much. You've already helped me by inviting me to stay at your house until I get this place in shape. I'll never be able to repay you, as it is."

"Yes, you can. You can go to church with me tomorrow morning."

"I–I don't know, Hank. I haven't been to church in a long time. I'm not sure God would even recognize me."

"I'll remind Him who you are. Say yes. You go to church with me, and I'll help you with the house. Can't beat a deal like that, can you?"

"Well—when you put it that way. I–I guess—"

"Okay, it's a done deal." Hank pulled off his coat and hung it over the back of a kitchen chair, then reached out his hand to assist her with her jacket. "I'm here to stay, Tink. Now where do we start?"

ða

Tina slipped out of her jacket, all the time eyeing the man who had come to her rescue so many times. How she'd dreaded coming to Juneau again. The thought of staying in a cheap motel and working on the house by herself had nearly kept her from fulfilling her grandmother's last request. But then she'd run into Hank and all of that had changed. She was staying in his beautiful home, and he was volunteering to help her with the renovation. "How can I be so lucky?"

"Hey, Kiddo, I'm the lucky one. I've got you back in my life."

They wandered from room to room, taking stock and making a list of the paint, scrapers, nails, screws, tools, and the other things they'd need for the job. At noon he drove to a nearby deli and brought back sandwiches, chips, and drinks, while Tina cleaned up the bathroom as best she could, putting out the new towels and washcloths and a fresh bar of soap she'd bought the day before.

The two settled themselves on the sofa, after pulling off the old sheets Gram had spread over it before leaving her beloved Juneau, ready to enjoy their impromptu lunch and good conversation. Both jumped when the phone began to ring.

Tina made a mad dash for it. "Hello."

"No. Not now. I'll call you back. I'm sorry. You'll have to wait. Just be patient. I'll phone you tonight. Good-bye."

"I forgot you'd had the phone turned on," he said, looking curious.

"Oh, I'd nearly forgotten too. It was some man from the lumberyard."

He frowned. "Lumberyard? I thought they closed at six. You said you'd call him back tonight."

Her brows lifted. "Oh? Did I say tonight? I meant tomorrow."

Her answer didn't seem to satisfy Hank, but she was glad he didn't ask any more questions.

"Remember those wonderful sandwiches your mom used to make for us?" Tina asked as she popped a potato chip into her mouth. "She'd load them up with slices of ham and cheese and lettuce. Umm, those were the best sandwiches I'd ever eaten. We didn't have sandwiches like that at our house. We barely had food of any kind."

"I also remember how much you loved her brownies."

"I always made a pig out of myself, didn't I?"

"I wasn't going to say that, but now that you've brought it up—"

Tina swatted at his arm. "As I recall you did a pretty good job on those brownies yourself!"

"We sure had fun, didn't we?"

"We sure did."

"Even this house brings back memories. I can remember

walking you here after school. Remember that tire swing?"

Tina jumped to her feet and rushed to the window, pulling the curtain aside and peering out. "It's gone!"

"The rope probably rotted years ago."

She let the curtain fall back in place with a sigh. "Probably. I was hoping it was still there. I loved that swing."

"Me too. I always planned to put one up when I had kids. Guess that'll never happen now."

The faraway look in his eyes spoke worlds, and it ripped at Tina's heart. "You'd have been a wonderful father, Hank."

"I like to think so. My dad was a great role model."

"My folks were lousy role models. I always wanted to be like your mom. She was the best. I know you miss her. And your dad too."

Hank checked the thermostat, lowering the setting a few degrees now that the house had begun to warm up, then, once again, took his place on the sofa. "I do miss them."

Tina pulled an old photo album from a shelf by the fireplace and blew the dust from its cover. "Wanna take a trip down memory lane with me? I'll bet our picture is in here."

Hank nodded and patted the seat beside him.

Carefully opening the brittle cover, Tina let out a giggle. "That's me! The day I was born."

"You sure were a scrawny little thing. But cute," he added quickly.

She gave him a frown, then looking back at the album, squealed with delight. "Look, here I am on my first birthday, eating a piece of birthday cake!"

He leaned in for a better look. "You're sure you're eating that cake? Looks more to me like you were mashing it into your face. What's the matter? Couldn't you find your mouth?"

Ignoring his teasing remark, she flipped to the next page. "Oh, Hank, that's you!" Her finger pointed to a chubby little boy sitting in a sand pile, playing with a red toy fire engine.

"Me? You really think that's me?"

"I know it's you. I'd recognize that smile anywhere."

Hank grinned. "Who's that pretty little girl with the doll?"

"Me, you silly. I was pretty then, wasn't I?"

"Not as pretty as you are now, Tink."

She smiled up at him. "No wonder you were always my favorite boy." She flipped another page. "There's your mom! I didn't know Gram took her picture."

"Me either. She looks happy there."

"Oh, Hank, look! Gram saved my first report card." She carefully lifted the yellowed folded piece of paper and peeked inside. "All A's."

"With grades like that, you should've gone on to college."

Her fingers pressed shut the card's cover as she stared off in space, reminded of less happy times. "I never planned to go to college, especially after my dad died. Mom had left me, and my grandmother sure couldn't afford to send me. All I could think about was graduating from high school and getting out of Juneau and away from the bad memories. You know, Hank, I always thought my mom and dad's six pack of beer meant more to them than I did. It seemed I was always in their way. I'm sure they both wished I'd never been born."

"Don't even think that!" Hank brushed a lock of hair from her forehead. "I knew you had it rough at home, but I really don't remember you complaining that much about it. Not even when I asked you about the bruises you always seemed to have on your arms and legs."

"What good would complaining do?" She shrugged. "I learned to live with it, as best I could. That seemed to be my only choice in life. At least until I was out on my own."

"How did the time get away from us? It seemed one moment we were kids playing in a sandbox, and the next minute we were seniors, graduating from high school. And look at us now. What happened, Tink?"

A feeling of melancholia swept over her. A heaviness that was indescribable. What a mess she'd made of her life. Nothing had turned out like she'd planned. What happened to all those dreams, those visions of success? "I don't know,

Hank. I honestly don't know."

She closed the album and placed it back where it belonged, but in so doing noticed a big cardboard box wedged into the bottom shelf of the bookcase. A box she couldn't remember ever seeing before. Stooping, she gave it a few tugs. It finally dislodged, and she was able to carry it to the coffee table.

Hank watched with interest. "Whatcha got there?"

"Probably more pictures."

There were two long strips of packing tape holding the lid in place. He pulled out his pocketknife and easily sliced through them before lifting the lid and setting it to one side.

Tina's fingers sifted through the hundreds of snapshots. "I have no idea who most of these folks are. Probably distant relatives. Oh, look. Here's my mom and dad's wedding picture!" She held it out for him to see. "They looked happy then, didn't they? Too bad they had to change. I rarely saw either my mom or my dad ever smiling like that. Most of the time they were either fighting or dead drunk."

Hank took the picture but remained silent.

"Oh, and here's a picture of Tippy, your dog. Remember how he'd fetch the newspaper for your dad?"

Hank reached for the picture. "I sure do. He was a great dog. He died of old age when I was off at college. I'm glad I wasn't here at the time. Mom said he had a pretty rough time of it at the last. I'd rather remember him as the feisty, active dog he was most of his life. I dread the day I lose Ryan."

"And here's one of our old house! I can't believe it was this small. A living room, one bedroom, a tiny kitchen, and a bathroom that barely held the bathtub. My condo in Chicago is a little bigger than this, and it's in the low-rent district. Of course I have to walk up three flights of stairs to get to it."

Hank laughed, then took the picture and stared at it for a long moment before putting it back in the box.

Tina rummaged her fingers through the myriad photos, finally pulling a large flat box from the very bottom.

"What's that?" Hank asked as she untied the ribbon and

lifted the lid. "More pictures?"

Her broad smile said it was something good, something familiar. "Valentines!" she told him excitedly as she pulled several handmade cards from the top of the pile and fanned them out across the table top.

Hank picked one up, read it silently, then handed it to her. "From one of your many admirers."

Tina read the verse. "From Charles Pickering. Funny, I don't remember Charles Pickering at all."

"I do. He was that skinny little kid who wore thick glasses. I think he sat behind me in arithmetic."

She lifted another valentine from the pile. "This one is from Caroline, my best friend."

Hank snickered as he took it from her. "I thought I was your best friend."

"She was my best girlfriend," Tina said, correcting herself. "And here's one from Mrs. Lindsey, our teacher. She was nice, wasn't she?"

"She sure was. She gave me A's when I deserved B's."

"Did not!"

"Did too!"

"Did not. You were one of the smartest boys in the class."

"You'd better say that. Isn't there a valentine in there from me? I always gave you a valentine."

Tina filtered through the stack of cards, calling out each sender's name as she shifted each one to the bottom of the pile. One of the very last ones was the one she was seeking. A beautiful heart, cut from red construction paper and trimmed with white paper flowers and white hand-cut hearts. Each one pasted on a bit askew, but nonetheless pretty. She smiled when she saw the handwriting. It was definitely that of a third-grade boy. "Oh, I like this one," she said waving it before him with a teasing smile. "Let me read it to you."

Hank covered his face with his hand. "That one looks very familiar. Mine. Right?"

"All I'm going to say is that this guy was a real poet." She began to read, exaggerating each word, enunciating it carefully, smiling at him at every pause. " 'Tink is pretty. Tink is smart. I'll love you forever. Here is my heart. Be My Valentine.' And it's signed, Peter Pan."

◈

Hank listened, remembering how he'd struggled to come up with words that rhymed. Poetry had never been his best talent, but he'd tried. "I meant it, you know," he said shyly.

"That I was pretty? And smart?"

He took her hand in his and gazed into her eyes. "Of course, but I really loved you. Or at least I thought it was love. My mom kidded me and told me it was puppy love."

She reached up and tenderly stroked his cheek. "And I loved you too. Actually, you're the reason I've never married. I've compared all men to you, and none of them ever measured up. You spoiled me, Peter Pan. You were perfect."

"Me, perfect? Hardly." Hank was sure he was blushing, something he hadn't done in a long time.

"You were to me."

He kissed the tip of her nose. "Ah, but you were young and impressionable. I still can't believe some big, handsome, intelligent man hasn't swept you off your feet and whisked you off to the altar."

"Not yet," she said softly, the smile disappearing from her face. "Not yet."

As Tina gathered the valentines from the table, Hank carefully folded the red heart in half and slipped it into his jacket pocket, along with the handmade envelope, unobserved, before rising and rubbing his hands together briskly. "We, my lady, had better get to work if you're going to have this place ready for your grandmother."

"Yes, Sir!" She gave him a half salute before sliding the lid onto the box and wedging it back into the bookcase shelf.

◈

Tina moaned and opened one eye as the buzzer sounded on the alarm clock on her nightstand. Every bone in her body ached.

Why she and Hank had worked at cleaning up Gram's house until ten she'd never know. But she had to admit, they'd made great headway. She glanced at the clock. Eight o'clock. That gave her an hour to shower, wash and dry her hair, and get dressed for the middle service at Hank's church. She'd been dead tired when they'd gotten home from Gram's and had gone right to bed. Why had she ever agreed to go with him?

A slight rap on the door made her throw back the covers and reach for her robe.

"Tina?" a male voice said in a whisper. "Time to get up."

One look at the mirror, and she knew there was no way she was going to open that door. "I'm up," she whispered back, her face pressed against the door. "Give me an hour, okay? I want to shower and wash my hair."

"You sleep okay?"

"Oh yes, much better than I did at that motel, thanks to you and your wonderful hospitality."

"I'll tell Faynola to have breakfast on the table about nine. We need to leave for church by nine-thirty."

She was about to tell him she'd changed her mind and would be working at the house all day, instead of going to church with him.

"Tina?"

"Yes."

"I'm glad you're going to church with me this morning."

"Ah—yeah, me too. Just don't expect me to make a habit of it."

෴

Hank sneaked a peek at his companion as they stood side by side, singing, and sharing a hymnal. She was every bit as beautiful as she'd been the day she'd graduated from high school, perhaps even more beautiful. Funny, he'd never really thought of her as beautiful back then. She was his good friend. The one he could count on to stand by him when he needed a helping hand, or encouragement. The one who'd cheered him on at football games, even when he'd fumbled the ball. The one who'd nominated him for class president, then had run his campaign. His buddy. His confidante. Nothing more.

When they sat down, he casually took her hand in his and gave it a slight squeeze. The smile she shot up at him melted his heart, and he had to admit, he hadn't had feelings like that since he'd spent time with Glorianna Kane. Nearly every day since his wife had died and he'd lost Glorianna, he'd asked God to bring another woman into his life, the woman of His choosing. Someone to share his home, his joys, his ups, his downs, his life, and all that he had. But God hadn't seen fit to answer, and he'd almost begun to think he'd be spending the rest of his life alone. Could Tina be that person? That one special woman God had for him? She'd come into his life so suddenly, so unexpectedly. They had much in common, and Tina would be a wonderful wife. He shook his head to clear his thoughts. But no matter how hard he tried, he couldn't get his mind off the lovely woman sitting beside him.

❧

Tina smiled up at Hank when he took her hand in his. It was like old times again. When she was five and learning to roller skate. She'd fallen down, hard, and Hank had come skating over quickly, concerned about her and offering his hand to help her up.

Then when she was in the ninth grade and tumbled down a flight of stairs at their school and all the other kids stood laughing at her clumsiness, it was Hank who told them all to shut up and reached out his hand to her. When she'd worn a borrowed dress to the junior prom because her mother couldn't, and wouldn't, buy her a new one, and one of the snooty girls had made fun of it, calling it ugly and old-fashioned, it was Hank, the most popular boy in school, who wiped away her tears and told her she was the prettiest girl there.

Hank had always been there for her. Dear, sweet, even-keel Hank. It was hard to imagine a woman, any woman, preferring another man to him. She'd never tell him, but all through high school she'd had fantasies about being Hank's girlfriend. But he'd never thought of her in any way except that of a friend. Now here she was with him again, staying in his home, working side by side with him at Gram's house, sitting next to him in church, and it felt good. Familiar. Cozy.

"I hope you'll come again next Sunday," Hank told her as he ushered her out to the foyer, nodding to friends and acquaintances, stopping now and then to shake hands and introduce Tina to his friends on the way to his SUV.

"Maybe. I have to admit I did enjoy the service." She gave him a slight nudge with her elbow. "I'd forgotten what a nice bass voice you have."

"You did pretty good harmonizing with me too. Remember how we used to sing that silly song about Old Aunt Jemima and the swimming hole? I learned it at Cub Scout camp and taught it to you."

Tina grinned. "Of course I remember it. We sang it often enough. It drove your mom crazy!"

"She was only teasing when she complained. She really liked it."

"Your mom was a good sport. She liked anything you did, and she was always nice to me. So was your dad."

"Yeah, my folks were tops. Even as a kid I knew it."

As he opened her door, a tall, good-looking bearded man hurried across the parking lot toward them. "Hey, Hank!"

Hank turned, then stuck out his right hand to the man who took it with a vigorous shake. "Hi, Claude. How goes it?"

"Fine, but I have a quick legal question for you, if you've got a minute."

"It'll only take a minute," Hank told to Tina. "Okay?"

She nodded, as he opened the car door and motioned her inside. She crawled in, waited until he'd closed the door, then sank back in her seat. *Good old Hank. I wonder how many other lawyers would take their personal time, on a Sunday morning, to dole out free legal advice?*

With her window closed against the cold morning air, she couldn't hear what they were saying. But from all appearances,

Hank was doing most of the talking. No doubt giving the man the legal help he was seeking. As she watched him smile and gesture with his hands, she saw not the stable, dependable, professional man he had become, but the handsome boy with whom she'd grown up. The boy she'd loved all her life. The boy she still loved. But it was too late. Even if Hank could ever feel the same way about her as she felt about him, it was too late. Much, much too late.

"Nice guy," he said as he opened the door and slid beneath the steering wheel. "I should've introduced you to him."

"I thought nice guys made appointments with their attorney at their office to ask for legal advice, instead of asking for freebies in a parking lot."

Hank's face took on a scowl. "He's not only a client, he's a good friend, Tink. He'd never take advantage of me. If I had a question about a minor plumbing problem, I'm sure he wouldn't expect me to arrange a house call, even though he owns the plumbing company I usually do business with." The scowl turned to a slight smile as he inserted the key in the ignition and the car roared to attention. "Besides, he's a brother in Christ. We're buds!"

"Ouch. Should have kept my mouth shut, but remember, Hank, I've lived in Chicago a number of years. There you pay for everything you get. There's no such thing as free advice."

He released the brake and pulled the lever into the drive position, and the car moved slowly into the line of traffic waiting to exit the parking lot. "Juneau has changed since you've been gone, that's for sure. But it's still pretty laid back, and folks around here are still low key. Don't ever hesitate to ask for help when you need it. Most folks are more than willing to run to your rescue."

She gave his arm a playful jab. "I've noticed."

After discussing several options for lunch, the two of them decided on Hank's favorite restaurant, the Grizzly Bear. Though the parking lot was crowded, they soon found an empty slot, and he easily maneuvered the SUV into it. Hank took Tina's hand as they walked toward the door.

A pleasant-faced woman met them at the entrance, a stack of menus in her hand. She rushed to throw her arms around Hank's neck. "Hank! Where've you been keepin' yourself? Me and Dyami was just talkin' about you the other night."

"Just been busy, Emily." He turned to Tina, once again taking her hand in his. "I want you to meet an old friend. In fact," he said, pausing, "you might remember Tina. She went to school with Trapper and me. She worked for awhile as a cashier in Anna's shop." Then turning to Tina, he said, "Tina, this is Emily. She owns the Grizzly Bear."

The woman cocked her head and smiled. "Surely this isn't that little girl who used to live down the street from you. The one who wore the long pigtails?"

Tina stuck out her hand. "It's me."

"Quit hugging my mother," a deep male voice ordered as a handsome, bearded man moved quickly past the woman and extended one hand toward Hank.

Hank took the man's hand, giving it a firm shake. "Hey, Guy. I wondered if you'd be here today."

The man looked slightly familiar to Tina, although it was hard to tell with that heavy head of black hair and the well-waxed handlebar mustache. It seemed everywhere she went with Hank, a multitude of friends and close acquaintants managed to appear out of nowhere.

"This has to be Tina. Remember me?" the man asked, a friendly smile peeking out from beneath the mustache, which wiggled as he talked. "I'm Trapper. Trapper Timberwolf."

four

She had a sudden urge to strike out at the man who'd hurt Hank so badly. How dare he call himself a friend? "Trapper. Of course I remember you. I just didn't recognize you at first," she said coolly. "Hank's told me all about you."

Trapper withdrew his hand quickly, his smile disappearing. "Oh, oh. I think I know what you mean."

Hank jumped between the pair. "Tink, I told you things were fine between Trapper and me now."

"He's right, Tina. Thanks to Hank's understanding and his willingness to forgive, which—" He paused, and she was sure the look he was wearing was one of guilt. "I was going to say, which was more than I think I could have ever done. He was willing to forgive me for probably inflicting the worse hurt possible on him."

"Only because I knew all along Glorianna was really in love with you, Old Buddy," Hank inserted, smiling, his hand still on his friend's shoulder. "I have to admit, it was only through God's help and a lot of prayer. What I really wanted to do was deck you and take my girl back, but I knew I'd only be fooling myself. You and Glorianna belong together."

"Did I hear my name?" an attractive woman asked as she wiggled her way in between the two men.

Hank slipped an arm about her waist and pulled her close, giving her a kiss on her cheek.

But before he could introduce her, Tina blurted out, "You must be Glorianna, the woman who hurt Hank so badly."

Glorianna stopped smiling. So did Trapper. And so did Hank.

"How could you do such a thing?"

"Look," Trapper said, his deep voice a mere whisper as he looked around at the other restaurant patrons standing near them, "why don't the two of you join us for lunch? We can continue our conversation there, instead of here in the lobby."

Eat with you? Tina wanted to shout out at the man. *Why would I want to spend any time with you and that woman? What you did to Hank was unforgivable!* But she kept her peace, not wanting to further embarrass Hank. She hoped he'd tell Trapper no, and they could either find another table or go to another restaurant.

"We'd love to have lunch with you and Glorianna," Hank said as he moved to Tina's side, his arm circling her waist. "Are the kids here?"

"Nope. Glori's mother and dad are here visiting for the week. They insisted the two of us have a nice, peaceful, kid-less lunch today. I think they're fixing hot dogs at home."

"Too bad," Hank said as the four of them moved toward the table, with Trapper's mother in the lead. "I wanted Tink to meet them."

Tina could feel her anger rising, and she had to bite her lower lip to keep from saying things she felt needed to be said. *Are these people all mad? When someone hurts you, you don't just forgive them and go on with life, pretending things are all rosy and hunky-dory. Hank, how can you be so congenial with these people?*

"Trapper, let's put Glorianna here, next to Tink," Hank told his friend as he pulled out Tina's chair. "I want them to get acquainted."

Tina gave Hank a glare, hoping he would get the message that she didn't want to get to know Glorianna. There was no way she could ever be friends with the woman, but Hank only smiled back. She considered faking a headache or rushing to the ladies' room on the pretense of becoming violently ill, wishing she were any place but sitting in the foursome at that table.

"Oh yes," Glorianna said as she slipped into the chair. "I do hope we can be friends. When Hank came over the other day and told us you were in town, well, we just thought it was wonderful. He was so happy he ran into you when he was returning that nightgown Trapper bought for me."

Trapper sat down and folded his long legs under the table. "Boy, was he ever. I was afraid I was imposing on him, asking him to exchange that gown for a smaller one, but he sure didn't see it that way. He even thanked me for asking him to do it when he told me about meeting you in the department store."

"I couldn't believe it was really Tink. It'd been years since I'd heard from her," Hank explained as he handed her a menu.

"Tink?" Glorianna muffled a giggle. "You call her Tink?"

"Long story. But yes, I've called her Tink since we were toddlers. She was a very special part of my growing-up years. My best friend," Hank explained.

"You're moving back to Juneau?" Trapper asked, picking up his menu.

Still miffed, Tina struggled to speak without letting her anger show, not for their sakes, but for Hank's. "Yes. My grandmother and I. I put her in a nursing home here in Juneau when we arrived. I go visit her at least once a day."

"Hank said—" Glorianna began, her gaze fastened on Tina. "He said your grandmother is dying? I'm so sorry!"

Despite her feelings of resentment, Tina found herself mellowing with each moment. Glorianna's concern for her grandmother seemed so sincere. So real. "Yes, the doctor says she may last six months, but it's doubtful. Her desire was to come back to Juneau. To die at home in the old house she and my grandfather shared for nearly fifty years."

"And you're getting her house ready?" Trapper asked with a smile that, too, seemed sincere and filled with concern. "I know Hank is helping you, but I'd be glad to help too. I'm gone most of the week on my job, but I'm free on weekends, and—"

"No, thank you," Tina said quickly. The idea of spending more time with these people did not set well with her at all. "Hank and I are managing, and the work is coming along quite nicely."

Hank grinned. "Actually, I think we're even a bit ahead of

where we thought we'd be when we first drafted out the renovation plans. But if we need you, I'll call you," he told Trapper, as he folded his menu and placed it on the table in front of him.

"That goes for me too, Tina." Glorianna warmly touched Tina's arm with the tips of her fingers. "With my folks here to look after the kids, I could help you this week. Maybe wash windows? Or clean out cupboards? I'd be glad to help in any way I can."

Am I in la-la land? Can all this nicey-nice stuff really be happening? Tina wondered as she looked at the three. *How can they ignore the awful thing that happened between them? Is this all an act? I'd think Hank would want to rip their heads off!*

"No. Thanks for your offer," she answered without enthusiasm, mustering up a weak smile, "but there really isn't anything for you to do right now."

"Maybe she could help you paint that hallway," Hank inserted.

Tina wanted to strangle him. "I'm sure you're much too busy. Didn't Hank say you inherited Anna's quilt shop? The Bear Paw?"

"She used to work for your aunt," Hank explained quickly, his gaze flitting to Tina, then back to Glorianna.

"Yes, I still own the shop. But once little Emily Anna was born, I knew being home with her like I'd been with my oldest son, Todd, was the most important thing in my life. As quickly as I could, I more or less phased myself out of it. Oh, I still keep a close watch on it and lend a helping hand now and then and teach a few classes. But Jackie Reid, the woman who managed the shop for Anna, pretty much runs things. She's made it possible for me to be right where I want to be—at home with my children."

I wish this woman wasn't so likable, Tina thought as she listened to her words. *She's not at all what I expected. Glorianna has values and is certainly not trying to make her mark in the world.*

The waiter arrived, took their order, then brought their dinner salads. Without preamble, each reached for one another's hand and Hank prayed.

"You've never married?" Trapper asked after the "amen."

Tina picked up her fork, wondering what other things Hank had told them about her. It seemed they knew much more about her than she did them. "No. Came close a few times, but realized I was more in love with love than I was with the man. I backed off before things got that far." She wanted to add, *You two should have backed off too, rather than hurt a fine man like Hank,* but kept her silence.

The three stole quick glances at one another, and she knew her words had made them uncomfortable. If they hit the mark, so much the better.

"Well, I guess that's to your credit," Trapper finally said, twirling his fork in his salad without meeting her eyes. "Mistakes are hard to unravel. There are consequences."

Tina nodded. "Yes, there certainly are."

"Look," Trapper said, putting down his fork and wiping at his mouth with his napkin, frustration showing on his face. "Let's just say it and get it over, instead of pussyfooting around. I, for one, would like to clear the air." He turned his full attention to Tina. "What I did to Hank was horrible. I admit it. If he'd done the same thing to me—well, I'm not sure what I would have done. I was stupid, Tina. I loved Glori right from the first day I met her. I knew it. She knew it. My parents knew it. But I was too stubborn to admit it to myself. And like an idiot, I was afraid to commit to her, knowing that commitment would change my life forever, and I liked my life exactly as it was. Or so I thought I did, until I nearly lost her to Hank."

Tina cast a quick look Hank's way, feeling like a spotlight was being focused on her, and she didn't like the feeling. But Hank sat quietly nibbling on his salad.

"Please try to forgive us, Tina," Glorianna said gently, after exchanging an adoring smile with her husband. "The last thing either of us wanted to do was hurt Hank. And don't blame Trapper. It was my fault. I loved Trapper, but I knew once he found out I was pregnant with my deceased husband's child, he would run the other way, and that's exactly what he did. Kind, understanding Hank showed up at my door when I needed someone in my life. I'd lost Trapper. I was new to Alaska. I was trying to run a business with no business experience, and there was Hank. Strong, intelligent, smart, witty Hank. But it wasn't like you think. I honestly cared for Hank. I still do! But in a different way than I did for Trapper. If I'd had any idea Trapper wanted to marry me, I would never have accepted Hank's proposal. I was as appalled as anyone when he burst into the church and gathered me up in his arms and carried me off. I fought him—"

"She sure did!" Trapper added, in his wife's defense. "I had the scratches and bruises to prove it."

"Someday," Glorianna told her, "you'll meet that special someone, and you'll want so much to spend the rest of your life with him, you'll do everything you can to make it happen. Then I think you'll understand a little better about our situation and why we behaved the way we did. You can't imagine how miserable we were about what we'd done to Hank."

Hank laid down his fork. "It's true, Tink. I was furious at first. When I caught up with them I was ready to kill Trapper. Well, not kill him, but I was going to maim him for life! But the minute I saw the two of them together, with Trapper holding Glorianna in his arms, her still in her wedding gown, I knew it was I who was wrong. Not them. I'd taken her from him when she'd been her most vulnerable. She was his. It was I, not Trapper, who stole the bride from her beloved."

"You're much too generous," Tina said, still chafing at the ordeal her friend had gone through.

Hank took her hand and squeezed it hard, his eyes penetrating hers. "Give it up, Tink. I have. Long ago. You were my best friend from the time we were in diapers, right up through high school. These two, along with you, are my best friends now. I don't want to give up any of the three of you. I know, if you give them half a chance, you'll learn to love them as much as I do. Please. Won't you try? For my sake?"

❧

Although tiring because of the work they were doing, the next few days were some of the happiest days Hank had known in a long time, working side by side with Tina, listening to the ring of her laughter, and exchanging smiles as they kidded one another.

Sometimes, as he sat at his desk trying to keep focused on the work he was doing for his clients, he found himself watching the clock. Looking forward to the evening when he would be with Tina. Scraping off old wallpaper, stripping layers of paint from the doors and woodwork, re-puttying drafty windows, cleaning rust stains from the bathtub and lavatory, and the myriad other chores that needed to be done to make Gram's house livable. He'd offered to lend her enough money to have the work done, since Tina's grandmother's money would probably be enough to pay for only the supplies and not much of the labor. But Tina wouldn't hear of it, saying her grandmother preferred to keep everything debt free.

Secretly, he was glad when she'd said no. If someone else was doing the work, there wouldn't be a reason for the two of them to spend evenings and weekends together. And besides, it made him feel good to actually do some physical labor. It sure beat spending big bucks to join a health club. Although he'd never had difficulty sleeping nights, now he was asleep the minute his head hit the pillow. Sometimes he was so tired after a day at the office and a night working at Gram's, he even considered forgoing his nightly shower.

Tina was hard at work, steaming the last bit of wallpaper in the back bedroom, when Hank arrived with a big bag of Chinese take-out for supper, and didn't even hear him come in. He placed the sack in the kitchen, then slipped up behind her, wrapping his arms about her waist. "You really ought to keep that front door locked. Anyone could come in here and snatch you up!"

She turned off the steamer and spun around in his arms, facing him, her face just a breath away. It was all Hank could do to keep from kissing her. "Looks to me like someone just did," she said with a grin, making no attempt to escape his grasp, her finger tapping the tip of his nose.

Hank could feel his heartbeat quicken as he gazed into her eyes. *Hold it, Boy. Take your time. She's given you no indication she wants anything more than your friendship. You don't want to get hurt again. Make sure this relationship is going somewhere before you make any advances.* Reluctantly, he loosened his grasp and backed away.

"Seriously, Tink, you need to be more careful. Juneau is a nice town, but like all major cities, it has its problems too. Please keep the door locked when I'm not here. And remember, you've got guys you don't even know working up on that roof this week."

"You're an old worrywart," she told him as she flipped the switch on the steamer and turned back toward the wall. "But I will."

He leaned over and pulled the plug from the receptacle. "Soup's on. Time to quit and have a little supper. Why don't you go wash up while I put things on the table? I'll bet you haven't eaten all day."

She grinned and pulled a wadded-up candy bar wrapper from her pocket and held it up before him. "Yes, I did. After I got back from visiting my grandmother. See!"

"Oh, terrific. Nourishing food." He grinned as she turned and tossed the wrapper into the big trash box in the middle of the floor.

After a wink, she disappeared into the bathroom. He had to laugh at her appearance. She looked nothing like the attractively dressed woman who went to church with him on Sundays. Her jeans had holes in the knees, her shirt had the pocket nearly ripped off, her tennies had paint spattered on them, she wore no makeup, and her hair was pulled back in a tight ponytail. But to Hank, she was still one of the most beautiful women he'd ever seen. What had happened to that average-looking little girl with whom he'd grown up? The one with the perpetually skinned knees and dirty face. The tomboy who could climb trees nearly as fast as he could. The one who carried frogs around in her pocket.

One thing was certain. That girl had changed. Outwardly, at least. Inside, he had a feeling she was the same caring, compassionate Tink he'd always known.

Hank pulled two clean plates and some silverware from the cupboard, added ice to two glasses, filled them with soft drink, and waited for Tina before sitting down. In minutes, she bounced into the kitchen wearing a clean shirt, the paint spatters gone from her face, except for one tiny spot on her forehead. Hank smiled at the transformation as the tip of his finger gently flicked off the offending blob of paint.

She giggled and swatted at his hand. "I tried! But one of our next projects had better be getting that new mirror up in the bathroom. Kinda hard to wash your face by feel."

His finger slid beneath her chin, lifting her face to his. "It looked kinda cute. I should've left it there."

"You!" She brushed his hand away and plopped into a chair, sighing. "I'm tired. You get to sit in that plush office all day, letting your secretary do the work, while I'm here slaving away."

"Hey, tomorrow is Saturday. My time's coming. Tomorrow you can sit in the chair and watch me work. You deserve a break."

She reached for an egg roll but drew her hand back quickly. "Guess you'll want to pray before we eat."

"Well, He has provided our food. Don't you think we ought to thank Him for it?"

"I guess. But if He provided it and you went after it, I'd better be grateful to both of you!"

Hank couldn't conceal his smile as he reached across the table and took both her hands in his, lifting his face heavenward. "Thanks, Lord, for this food we are about to eat. Thank

You for the strength and desire You've given Tink as she's set about on this monumental task of getting her grandmother's house ready for her. And thank You most of all for bringing Tink back into my life. Amen."

For only a brief moment, Hank thought he detected a tear in Tina's eye. It had to be because he'd mentioned her grandmother's illness, but he hoped it was more than that. From all appearances, it seemed to him Tink had turned her back on God. As a Christian, Hank was concerned for her. Although he had to admit at times he, too, had thought God had deserted him. Especially in the dark of the night, when his life had become unbearably stressful because of Sheila's cancer. Sometimes instead of turning to God, he'd given up to despair and shaken his fist at Him. Challenging Him to spare her life, if He was real, and truly a God of love. God hadn't seen fit to do that. Instead, He'd taken his precious wife from him. Other times, he'd felt God's presence and known He was in control. That taking Sheila was part of His overall plan. That even though he could see no valuable purpose in it, through prayer and God's Word, he'd been able to face it all and praise God instead of blaming Him. Now, looking back, he wondered how he could have ever doubted God and His wisdom.

"Hank."

He suddenly realized he was still holding on to both of Tina's hands and she was smiling that little mischievous smile at him across the table. "Sorry. Guess my mind wandered."

Her smile disappeared. "From the look on your face, it must've wandered to something unpleasant. Want to talk about it?"

"I–I was thinking about Sheila."

Tina pulled her hands from his and opened the little carton of sweet and sour pork, forked out a few pieces, then reached the container toward him. "I wish I'd known her."

Hank absentmindedly took a few pieces from the carton. "Me too. She was a real lady."

She opened the box of chi tan chuan and placed two of the

egg rolls on her plate before handing the little box to him. "I know you loved her, but somehow I can't see you living the rest of your life alone."

"At first, I thought I'd never be able to even consider having another woman in my life, but time changes that perspective. You get lonely. You see couples holding hands, walking in the park with their kids, and your heart aches to have a wife and children of your own. You work at your job and make good money doing it, but for what?"

"I'm sorry things didn't work out with Glorianna."

He opened the lid on the carton of niu ju chin jow and pushed it across the table. "But what about you? At least I've had a wife I adored. How come you've never married?" He forced a grin. "And don't say it was because you compared all men to me. I don't believe that for one minute."

Tina dabbed the paper napkin at her lips as she smiled and leaned back in her chair. "I've dated a number of men, Hank. I've honestly tried to find the right man, but I'm afraid I've been a lousy judge of character. The guys I thought were decent turned into long-armed monsters. You have no idea what a woman is expected to do in return for a nice dinner and a movie these days. To put it plain and simple—I preferred not to have the hassle."

"Good for you." Hank smiled, then gave her an incredulous look. "Surely you're kidding me about the guys you've met."

"Nope, I'm not kidding. You've never lived in a place like Chicago. Men are different there, at least the men I met. After having a few of my first dates turn into a battle, I soon learned to just say no and not take any chances. I found the easiest way to avoid a wrestling match was to avoid dating altogether. Sad, isn't it, that you can't trust most men."

"So you've never found that one special man?"

"The women there are different too," she went on, ignoring his question. "Oh, not all of them, of course, but most of them seem to accept the fact that they're going to have to—" She paused, as if not sure how much explanation was needed.

"I get the picture."

Tina's face brightened. "Let's drop this subject and talk about more pleasant things."

"Like?"

"Like—what do you do for fun? When you're not helping damsels in distress remodel their grandmother's homes, that is. Surely you have interests other than lawyering."

"Lawyering?" A smile tilted his lips. "Is that a word?"

"It is in my dictionary."

He became thoughtful. "What other interests do I have? Well, let me see. Occasionally I fly up into the bush with Trapper and help him with his ministry to the bush people."

Her eyes opened wide as her jaw dropped. "Trapper is a missionary?"

"His main job is flying his seaplane for a number of major clients who have him on retainer. The rest of the time, he's a self-supporting missionary. He takes medicines and supplies to the people, that sort of thing. He and another missionary friend of his, a doctor. Sometimes Glorianna and the children go along. She takes fabric and teaches the women to make little things she can sell in her shop, to give them some badly needed money."

"It isn't hard for you to spend time with them? After what they did to you?"

"No, not at all! I wish you'd believe me," he said emphatically. "I love them both, and I love their children. I'm happy they include me in their lives."

"Hank Gordon. You're one in a million. Why didn't I meet someone like you, instead of all those Neanderthals? If I had, I might not—"

Hank waited a moment for her to finish her sentence, but when she didn't, he flashed her a smile, shrugged, and tore open one of the two fortune cookies that came with his order. He unfolded the tiny piece of paper and, reading to himself, tried to conceal the smile that threatened to erupt. *The love you have been searching for may be right under your nose.*

Eagerly, Tina unfolded hers and read aloud with a laugh, " 'Confucius say, man who live in glass house shouldn't run around in holey underwear.' " She turned to Hank. "What does yours say?"

Hank fumbled for words as he folded the tiny piece of paper and carefully slipped it into his pocket, saying the first thing that popped into his head. "Some coincidence, huh? It says the same thing as yours."

"Yeah, some coincidence," she said casually, as she began to clear the table. "I love those fortune cookies. It's amazing how many times their sayings are right on target."

Remembering the words printed on the one he'd slipped into his pocket, Hank asked, "You don't really believe in that sort of stuff, do you?"

She stacked his plate on top of hers before picking up their glasses, chop sticks, and plastic forks. "No, of course not! But you have to admit they're fun to read."

Hank fingered the tiny slip of paper in his pocket. "Yeah. Fun."

"I'll put these dishes in the sink and wash them later. I want to finish painting that trim around the pantry door before I clean up my brush. Then I want to start taking everything out of the kitchen cupboards and sort out what we'll keep and what we'll throw away."

Hank gathered up the little paper cartons and tossed them into the large trash can. "Sounds good. I'm going to work on that loose board on the front porch." He picked up his tool pouch and strapped it about his waist before slipping on his jacket and gloves. "Holler if you need me."

She nodded. "I will."

He located the loose board, then remembered he'd left his bag of nails on the table in the front hall. He pushed open the front door and found Tina hovered over the telephone, her back to him, speaking softly to someone on the other end. He picked up the nail bag and was backing out the door, when suddenly she began to speak more loudly and he caught her words.

"No! Don't! Not now. I'm not ready! I don't care. Listen to me. The time is not right. I want to get Gram's house ready first."

Hank stared at her. She seemed agitated. No, not agitated, angry. But why? And to whom was she speaking? She barely knew anyone in Juneau, especially not well enough to talk to them in such a terse manner. He stood silently, debating whether he should withdraw or offer to help with whatever was wrong. But Tina seemed to sense his presence and turned quickly toward him, giving him no choice. The look on her face was like that of a child who'd been caught doing something forbidden.

"I'll talk to you later," she said curtly into the phone before hanging it in its cradle.

"Anything wrong?" Hank asked with concern, not wanting to embarrass her by letting her know he'd overheard her conversation.

"No," she said, taking on a smile, "just a telemarketer. Makes you wonder how they got this number."

From the way she turned away from him and started fumbling with her hair, he knew she'd prefer to keep whatever that conversation was about to herself, and he wasn't about to press. He held up the bag. "Forgot my nails."

"And I'd better get back to the cupboards."

Hank watched as she moved into the kitchen. Something wasn't right with Tina. But what? This was the second time he'd caught her talking angrily to someone on the phone, and she'd made light of it both times. But from the look on her face, whoever was on the other end of that phone was saying something that upset her. What was Tink keeping from him?

⁂

Tina held her breath as she walked away. It wasn't right to keep this from Hank, but what choice did she have? He'd never understand. And she certainly didn't want any lectures!

No, I'm doing the right thing. Hank is a reasonable man. I can explain things to him later, just not now. I should never have taken him up on his offer to stay at his home. If I'd said no and hadn't accepted his offer to help me fix up Gram's house, he would never have had to find out. Things would have gone as planned, and no one would have been hurt. But no. I'm as vulnerable to Hank now as I was in high school. I couldn't resist the chance to be around him again. To be a part of his life. Even if just for a little while. Dumb! Dumb! Dumb! She rinsed the dishes and put them in the sink, barely aware of what she was doing.

"That didn't take long."

Still wrapped up in her thoughts, Hank's voice startled her as he came into the room, and she dropped a glass on the floor, shattering it over the discolored linoleum, and she began to cry.

He maneuvered quickly through the broken glass and wrapped her in his arms. "Don't cry, Tink. I'm sorry. I thought you heard me come in the front door."

"I–I'm sorry, the glass, I mean—it was my fault—I—"

"Your fault? Who's blaming you? And what difference does it make? It was an accident. If anyone's at fault, it's me. But who cares? It was just an old jelly glass. You can probably buy them at the thrift store for a dime apiece. It's certainly not worth crying over." He rested his chin in her hair.

It felt so good to be close to him. For a moment she forgot all the reasons she shouldn't be in his arms. "I'm sorry," she told him, her voice a near whisper. "I guess all of this remodeling is getting to me."

"You've taken on a big task and are doing far more than originally planned. We can still hire someone to come in here and finish this, if you're not up to it."

She lifted watery eyes to his, a tear running down her cheek. "It's what I'm doing to your life that upsets me, Hank. You haven't had a minute to yourself since I arrived."

His thumb brushed away the tear. "Have you heard me complaining? Having you come back to Juneau is the best thing that's happened to me in a long time. I'm afraid, since losing Glorianna, I've dug a hole for myself. Except for the happy times I've spent with Trapper's family, it seems all I've done is work. Or sit at home nights and watch ball games on TV. Oh, Sundays I go to church, but that's about it. But now with you here, my life has a purpose, and I'm loving every minute of it."

"Y—you're sure?" she asked between sniffles. "You're not just saying that to make me feel better?"

"Cross my heart. There's no place I'd rather be than right here, helping you get this place ready for your grandmother. Honest."

"Well—"

"It's your call. Do we get busy and finish fixing this place, or do we call a contractor and his crew of professionals to finish it faster than the two of us can? I'll still put up the money, if you want to get it done in a hurry."

"No, I can't let you do that. I've done a lot of strange things in my life, but going into debt isn't one of them. I won't use your money."

"You won't be in debt. I won't even charge you any interest, and you can pay me back when you can. There's no hurry."

"But I'd be indebted to you. Is that so much different?"

He doubled up his fist and touched a gentle blow to her chin. "For one, I volunteered; you didn't twist my arm. Two, I told you I need the exercise, so you're doing me a healthy favor. And three, I want to be here. I enjoy working with my hands, and being with you is the bright spot of my day. Until you came, I'd been pretty much stuck in a rut. If there's any indebtedness, it's on my part. You've made a new man out of me, and I like the feeling."

Her tear-stained face brightened as she looked up into his eyes. "Bet you think I'm a big baby."

"No, not a big baby. You're a caring woman with a lot of responsibility on her shoulders. Your job, your grandmother, undertaking this renovation. And from the looks of it, you've carried all that responsibility alone. You deserve a good cry."

"Thanks." She pushed away from his grasp and wiped her

eyes on the tail of her paint-stained shirt. "I'm glad you understand. Some people think I'm crazy to come back up here, even for awhile."

"I can't imagine anyone saying that about what you're doing. You've got a good heart, Tink. You always have had. I can't say I'm the least bit surprised by what you're doing for your grandmother." He didn't ask, but he wondered who those folks were she was speaking about. They didn't sound like the kind of friends Tina would have, and she no longer had parents to criticize her actions.

"Thanks, Hank. Your support is important to me."

"How was your grandmother feeling today when you visited her?"

"You know Gram. She let on like she was fine, but the nurse told me she'd had a terrible night. But she's happy to be back in Juneau and continues to smile." With one more quick wipe at her eyes, she backed off and began fidgeting with the broken handle on one of the cabinets. "I'd better remember to get another handle next time we go to the lumberyard."

Hank watched her with great interest. He was growing fonder of Tink each day, but her mood swings troubled him. One minute she was flitting around the old house, smiling and singing. The next, she was distant, spacey, as if somehow there was an invisible wedge between them, and it unnerved him. At first he'd assumed her melancholia was simply shyness. After all, it'd been years since they'd seen one another. Other times, it seemed her body was in Juneau, but her mind was somewhere else. Then there were the mysterious phone calls. Not one time had she ever told him who was on the other end. What was going on in Tina Taylor's life? And why did she choose to hide it from him?

Hank tried to put the out-of-character episodes from his mind, blaming them on Tina's weariness from the overwhelming job she'd undertaken. From the beginning, he'd been going out of his way to do things to make her happy. Bringing flowers unexpectedly. Buying her favorite candy.

Treating her to hot fudge sundaes after a long day of working at the house. Each time, her rewarding smile would make it all worthwhile. But then he'd overhear her on the phone or hear her crying long after the lights had all been turned out and she'd gone to bed, and he'd feel so helpless. *Tink, what is going on with you?*

ཉ

Saturday afternoon, as the two of them were working at the house, there was a rap on the door. Hank had just entered the living room in search of his coffee cup when he heard it. "I'll get it," he hollered out to Tina, who was putting the final piece of shelf liner in one of the newly painted kitchen cabinets.

Ryan rushed to the closed door and sniffed at it, a low growl rumbling through his chest. Hank pushed him aside and pulled open the door, expecting to see a friend from church who'd come to check on their progress or one of the neighbors coming by to introduce themselves. But the tall, slim, long-haired, bearded man, clothed head-to-toe in black leather, a skull attached to a long silver chain dangling from his ear, was definitely neither of those. "Yes?" Hank said apprehensively, glad Tina had thought to engage the lock on the storm door. "Is there something I can do for you?"

"Tina here?" the stranger asked, looking past him as he spat on the newly scrubbed front porch.

Hank's eyes widened. "Tina? Ah—sure—she's here."

"Who is it, Hank?" Tina called out from the kitchen.

Hank stared at the man, unable to believe Tina would have anything to do with someone of his sort. "Does Tina know you?"

The man hitched up his leather pants with a gloved hand and grinned at Hank, revealing two shiny gold front teeth. "She sure does. Me and her is engaged. We're gonna be married!"

five

Tina came into the living room, a dish towel in her hands. "Who was it?"

"I—ah—" Words seemed to fail Hank as he continued to stare at the man.

Knowing from the startled look on Hank's face something was radically wrong, Tina hurried to the door. Her heart felt as though it'd dropped into her shoes as her eyes locked with the caller's. "Lucky? Wh–what are you doing here?" The last person she expected to see, or wanted to see, at her door at such an inopportune moment was Lucky Wheeler.

The man smiled toward Tina and reached for the door handle. "Aw, my little sweetie, you really didn't want me to stay away, did you?"

Tina turned quickly toward Hank, who appeared immobilized, his face ashen, his gaze darting from Tina to the man and back again, as if he was in a state of shock.

"I told you I'd let you know when the time was right for you to come!" she said sharply, turning to face the man. She couldn't keep the raw edge from her voice. Why would Lucky forge on ahead when he knew she wasn't ready for him yet? "You should have listened to me."

"But I missed you, Baby," he said, tugging his collar up about his neck. "Aren't you gonna to let me in? It's cold out here. I ain't used to this Alaskan air. Come on, unlock the door."

Hank, finally seeming to find his voice, grabbed Tina's wrist as she reached for the little lever to unlock the door. "You—you really know this man?"

She nodded, her heart aching for deceiving Hank, after all he'd done for her. Why hadn't she gone ahead and told him about Lucky right at the start? Looking back, she'd been stupid to even think she could keep the two of them from meeting one another. "Yes," she stammered, "I know him."

Hank looked as if he was about to explode. "Surely he's not telling the truth! This has got to be some kind of joke! You aren't really planning to marry this man, are you?"

Tina sucked in a fresh breath of air, floundering for the right words to say to help soften the blow Hank had just been delivered. "Nearly," she said quietly, avoiding his eyes. "I haven't said yes yet."

"Surely you're not serious, Tink!" Hank grabbed her by the shoulders, ignoring the man at the door. "You haven't said a word about a boyfriend!"

"Well, I am her boyfriend, and a cold one at that!" The impatient man gave several hard yanks on the door handle. "Are you guys gonna open this door and let me in? I already let the taxi go, and it's a long walk back into town."

Hank stepped back out of the way, releasing Tina, and said, rather harshly, "I think you'd better open the storm door."

She pushed past him, released the lock, and Lucky thrust his long body through the opening, slamming the door shut behind him. "Whew, I thought Chicago was cold! Got any hot coffee in this place?"

Tina cast a quick glance at Hank, then back to Lucky. "Yes, in the kitchen. I just made a pot."

Ryan sniffed at the man's heavy black leather boots.

With a sudden move, Lucky landed a swift kick to the dog's head, sending him sprawling and yelping in pain.

"Hey, there!" Hank hollered as he quickly bent over the dog. "What was that for?"

"Don't like dogs. Never have," the man said arrogantly, as if his dislike for dogs gave him the right to mistreat them. "He shouldn't have been sniffin' around me like that."

Hank sent a questioning look toward Tina, but remained silent.

"You shouldn't have done that, Lucky!" Inside, she was seething at his uncalled-for behavior. His actions only made it harder for her to explain his presence to Hank. "Come on, I'll get your coffee," she told him as she made her way to the kitchen, leaving Hank still bent over Ryan.

Lucky tugged off his black leather gloves and rubbed his hands together briskly as he followed her, seemingly unconcerned about the damage he may have inflicted upon the dog.

Tina took a cup from the cupboard, filled it to the brim with steaming hot coffee, and handed it to him. "Why, Lucky? Why did you have to come now? I told you to wait!"

"I missed you, Babe. I thought I'd come on and help you with your grandma's house." He took a big swig, then smacked his lips together loudly. "Mm, mm, good coffee."

"But I told you to wait."

"Because of Lover Boy?" He gestured toward the doorway.

She glanced toward the living room, then answered in an almost whisper through gritted teeth. "No, he's not the reason. I wanted to have the house ready first. I thought we'd agreed you'd stay in Chicago until I told you to come."

He gave her a reproving look. "You didn't tell him about me, did you?"

She shook her head. "No. The time never seemed right. But if I'd known you wouldn't listen to me and were planning to come on ahead—"

Hank appeared in the doorway, his face still an ashen white. "Any more of that coffee left?"

Tina forced a smile, although the last thing she felt like doing was smiling. "Sure, let me pour you a cup. How's Ryan?"

"Okay, I hope. I put him in the bedroom and shut the door."

"Come over here and have a chair," Lucky ordered, as he eyed Hank suspiciously. "You and me need to get acquainted."

Hank seated himself next to the man and took the cup from Tina's hands.

"Guess Tina didn't tell you about me," Lucky said boastfully, with a near sneer. "Why am I not surprised?"

"No, I guess she didn't."

"I wanted to, Hank. Honest I did," Tina said defensively,

wishing this whole scenario could have been avoided, and if the two men had to meet, it would have been under better circumstances. "It's just—I mean—we were so busy with the house—and—"

"You should've told me, Tink. You shouldn't have kept this from me."

Knowing he was right, but hating to admit it, even to herself, she poured herself a cup of coffee, then dropped into a chair between the two men. "Yes, I should have. I owe you both an apology."

"Well, mine will have to wait." Lucky stood quickly to his feet. "Where's your bathroom?"

Tina gestured toward the hallway. "Second door on your left."

"You're sure that mutt's locked in?"

Hank's retort was icy cold. "Yes, I made sure he was safely locked in, so he wouldn't get kicked again."

Lucky threw back his head with a laugh that set Tina's teeth on edge. It was as though he deliberately wanted to cause trouble for her, and she couldn't understand why. Unless he was miffed because she hadn't told Hank about their relationship.

She waited until she heard the bathroom door close, then leaned toward Hank. How could she ever make him understand? "I wouldn't blame you if you never forgave me. I should've told you about Lucky."

"You mean about Lucky and you, don't you?"

She could tell by his tone her deception had hurt him deeply. "Yes, about Lucky and me. But it's not what you think—"

"You mean he's lying about the two of you being engaged?"

Her fingertips rubbed at her forehead, at the beginnings of a whopper of a headache. "Yes. I mean no. I mean—it was never settled. Lucky thinks we're going to be married, but I've never actually said yes or no."

"But you must've given him some indication." He glanced down the hallway before continuing. "I distinctly remember asking you if you'd ever had a special man in your life."

"You did ask me, but I never answered you."

"Look, Tink. I don't know anything about that man, but I can tell you one thing, he'd better not kick my dog again!"

The sudden sound of the toilet flushing, the running of water, and the bathroom door opening caused their conversation to come to an abrupt stop.

"Hey, Hank," Lucky said as casually as if he were talking to an old friend. "I hear Tina's been staying at your house. Got another empty bed?"

Now Tina's jaw dropped. "Lucky!"

"Well, does he?" he asked, turning to her with raised brows.

"You'll have to get a motel," Tina shot back, shocked at Lucky's audacity. "Or sleep on the floor here. We could put down a few blankets. I got rid of the old broken-down mattress. Since I haven't gotten around to papering Gram's room, I haven't bought a new one yet."

"Well, since I ain't got no money to pop for a motel room and I sure ain't gonna sleep on no floor, guess I'll have to stay over at old Hank's place with the two of you." Lucky plopped back down in the chair and stuck out his empty cup. "At least until I get me a job. Motels are expensive."

"I'll pay for the motel," Tina said, knowing the money she'd set aside to live on until the house was ready for occupancy was dwindling every day. This was an expense she hadn't planned on. If she'd known Lucky was going to pull this stunt, she would've kept Gram's old bed instead of giving it to the rescue mission.

"No, it's okay. Lucky can stay at my house. No sense paying for a motel. I've got plenty of room." Hank swallowed hard, then added, "I'm sure the two of you'll want to be together."

Tina's mouth tightened. After what Lucky had done to Ryan, Hank was willing to open his home to him? Unbelievable!

"Okay," Lucky said, setting his empty cup back down on the table. "Then it's settled. I don't know about the two of you, but I'm bushed. Can we call it a day now? I need me a couple of beers and a bed real bad, and in that order. It's been a long day."

"Oh?" Hank asked, picking up Lucky's cup and carrying it

and his own cup to the sink. "What time did you leave Chicago?"

Lucky let out a loud snort. "Time? Or day?"

Hank frowned. "Time or day? What do you mean?"

"Well, I left Chicago four days ago. Got into Seattle late yesterday. Flew from there this morning."

"Surely you didn't ride your Harley all the way to Seattle! You hitchhiked, didn't you?" Tina asked, eyeing the man as she poured the remainder of her coffee into the sink.

"You bet. Would've hitched from Seattle here too, but since that weren't possible, I grabbed me a flight. Took nearly everything I had in my pocket to pay for it," he explained, adding a few cuss words for emphasis. "And here I am!"

Hank pushed his empty chair up close to the table and stepped aside. "So you are."

ə

The ride to Hank's house would have been silent if it hadn't been for Lucky's constant chatter as he filled them in on each of the drivers and rigs he'd hitched with on his way to Seattle. Tink hung on the men's every word, even though he was using words Hank would just as soon never be used in a lady's presence. *What's with this woman? She's not acting at all like the Tink I thought I knew.*

Hank sighed with relief when the car finally came to a stop inside his garage. The three of them piled out.

"Hey, Hank Old Boy, you got yourself quite a spread here. Guess bein' a lawyer, you took some big old rich guys for a cleanin'. No wonder you lawyers have such a bad name."

Hank fought the desire to bounce back with a remark about guys who can't even afford a plane ticket, but decided nothing would be gained by exchanging snide words with the man. "It's not exactly a spread, as you call it, but I like it."

"That wasn't a very nice thing to say, Lucky, after Hank was good enough to invite you to stay at his home," Tina called back over her shoulder as she stepped into the large mudroom just off the kitchen.

Invite? Hank set his jaw. *I didn't invite him. He invited him-self! I just agreed for your sake!*

"What is it they say about lawyers?" Lucky asked with a chuckle as he followed at Tina's heels. "Deep down, they're pretty nice guys? About six feet deep down."

Hank's blood boiled as Lucky's laugh boomed out.

Tina turned and gave the rude man a chafing look. "Lucky, stop it! That remark was uncalled for!"

"Hey, I didn't give lawyers a bad rap. They gave it to themselves by takin' a big cut of everybody's money."

"I'm afraid you don't know much about me, Mr. Wheeler," Hank began, for some unknown reason feeling he needed to defend himself. "I would never take advantage of a client."

Lucky whirled around to face him with a mocking scowl. "You expect me to believe that one? How about them big fees you charge? This house must've set you back a pretty penny."

"I only charge the going rate. And much of my work is pro bono."

Lucky gave him a blank stare. "What's that mean?"

"It means," Tina inserted, with a tug at his arm, "Hank does free work for those who can't afford to pay him."

"You've got to be kiddin'," he told Hank, pulling away from her grasp and adding a few more cuss words. "There ain't nuthin' in this world that's free. Somebody must give you a kickback under the table, right?"

"No!" Hank answered firmly, closing the door behind him before taking off his coat. "No kickbacks. I like doing it. It's my way of giving back to the community, and I look at it as a service to God."

Lucky's hands went to his hips. "Don't tell me you're one of those God freaks!"

Tina tugged on his arm again. "Lucky. Let it rest!"

"It's okay, Tink."

"No, it's not okay," she said with a stomp of her foot. "We're guests in your home. We have no right to talk to you like that!"

Lucky slipped an arm about her waist. "We? You got a frog in your pocket, Honey?"

"You," Tina corrected with a targeted punch of her forefinger to his chest, "are being just plain rude!"

The repugnant man glared at her. "You should've told this man about us, Tina. What's the matter? Ashamed of me because I don't wear designer suits like your boyfriend?"

"Hank's been very good to me, and he's not my boyfriend!" she shot back in an almost scream.

"Been kinda cozy, I'll bet, with just the two of you alone in this big house!" Lucky shot back. "I'd like to have been a little mouse and watched!"

"I–I'm sorry to interrupt." Faynola appeared in the mudroom doorway with Ryan at her side. "It's the phone for you, Mr. Gordon. It's Mr. Timberwolf. He's calling from Anchorage."

Hank turned to Lucky, his face filled with anger. "That remark was ridiculous and totally improper, Mr. Wheeler, and as long as you're in my home, I'd prefer you refrain from using swear words. I have to get the phone, but believe me, we'll discuss your rude comment later. And keep your distance from my dog! This is his home too."

Lucky gave a snort, then, in a mimicking, falsetto voice, said to Hank's back as he left the room, "But believe me, we'll discuss your rude comment later."

❧

"Enough, Lucky!" Tina gave him an exasperated look. "For your information, the two of us have not been staying alone in this house. Faynola is Hank's full-time housekeeper." Lucky's degrading mocking made her want to slap him.

"Oh, but what happens after the lights go out at night?"

Tina had had enough. "Just when I think you've changed, you pull a trick like this! I wish—"

"You wish I'd never come and interrupted your tea party?"

She blinked hard and pressed her lips together, trying to remember the good things about the man. "I was about to say, I wish you'd grow up and behave like a gentleman."

"Mr. Gordon said you'd be staying in the guest room," Faynola said, keeping her distance from the two. "I've put fresh towels on the foot of the bed. If you need anything else—"

"Thank you, Faynola." Tina forced back her anger and smiled at the woman.

"Dinner will be on the table at six."

"Hey, Fannie, how about a big, juicy steak?" Lucky asked, licking his lips. "I ain't had a nice steak in a long time."

"And you're not having one tonight!" Tina said angrily. "You'll have whatever Faynola is preparing!"

Lucky shrugged. "Well then, maybe we can have steak tomorrow night. How about it, Farina?"

"Her name is Faynola, Lucky."

"I'll take the steaks out of the freezer in the morning and marinate them for dinner," the housekeeper said, backing away. "Tonight we're having fresh salmon."

"Not one word!" Tina cautioned as Lucky's nose wrinkled up. "You're a guest in this house. It's about time you began to behave as one."

"You've sure gotten high and mighty since you left Chicago."

"Not high and mighty, Lucky. It's just that I'd almost forgotten how nice the folks in Alaska can be. Things are different here, and if you're going to stay, you'll have to change your ways, or you'll never fit in."

"Who says I want to fit in?"

Hank hurried back into the room and pulled his jacket off the hook. "Well, it looks like you two are going to have to eat dinner alone. Trapper is stuck in Anchorage, and the Boy Scout Father and Son Banquet is tonight. He's asked me to stand in for him and go with Todd."

"This another one of your bongo bongo things?" Lucky asked with a deriding laugh.

"It's pro bono," Hank said quietly, but his eyes had fire in them. "And no, I'm doing this as a favor for a friend. I hate to run off and leave—"

"We'll be fine," Tina inserted quickly, almost relieved the

two men wouldn't have an opportunity to finish the conversation they'd started. "Enjoy your evening with Todd."

"I will. I know Mr. Wheeler is eager to get a good night's rest, so I'll see you two in the morning. If you need anything, just ask Faynola."

Lucky grinned. "Lead me to the fridge. Right now, all I need is a couple of ice cold beers!"

"Sorry, Pal," Hank called back over his shoulder. "No beer in this house. Period!"

❧

"Where'd you disappear to?" Tina stared at Lucky with a scowl as he came back into the room. "Where did you get that beer? You know what Hank said! There was to be no beer in his house, and he meant it!"

"I was a mite thirsty, so while you and Farina was gettin' supper on the table, I walked to that gas place down the street and bought me a six-pack. Don't get your feathers all riled up. I won't let him see them!" he told her as he placed two cans on the table.

"I wondered why you'd left the room. I couldn't imagine what'd happened to you. Now I know!" She glared at him as she pointed a finger in his face. She wanted to throttle him for going against Hank's wishes like that. "Take those cans and the other four to the garage, and put it in that big trash barrel. You cannot bring that stuff into Hank's house!" she stated firmly, hoping her message was coming through loud and clear. But she knew from the look on his face, it wasn't going to be that easy to get him to get rid of that vile stuff.

He sat back down at the table. "Well, la-de-da! Excuse me, Miss Prissy! Who named you queen? I'll take them to the trash when I finish with them."

Tina ignored his remark, and they ate in silence. Finally, she placed her napkin on the table. "For a man who turned up his nose when he heard we were having fresh salmon for dinner, you sure cleaned up your plate. How many servings have you had?"

Lucky reached for another dinner roll, his fifth. "I was hungry, that's all."

"Oh? You didn't like the salmon?"

"Sure wasn't as good as a nice, thick, juicy steak." He slathered butter over his roll, dropping a blob on the tablecloth. "But I'm sure lookin' forward to that steak tomorrow night."

"This isn't a restaurant. You can't tell Faynola to——"

"Hey, she offered."

"Only because you put her on the spot. And that's another thing. We can't expect Hank to furnish our meals, as well as our housing. He's been nice enough to allow us to stay here, and——"

He shoved a big hunk of roll into his mouth. "He's been feeding you every night, hasn't he?"

She nodded, wishing he'd chew with his mouth closed. "Yes, he has, but you're here now. That makes a big difference. One extra person was asking a lot. Two is ridiculous."

He reached across the table, taking the remains of Tina's roll from her plate. "Why? That Farina woman has to fix his supper. All she has to do is add another potato to the pot and put a few more of them green things in the salad bowl."

"Her name is Faynola, not Farina. It'd be nice if you'd be courteous enough to at least call her by her right name."

"Well, hoop-de-do! How'm I supposed to remember?"

"Both of us staying here is an imposition on Hank's magnanimous generosity and hospitality."

"Oh, using more hoity-toity words on me, huh?"

She bit at her lower lip and gave him a harsh stare. "You know very well what I mean."

"Yeah, I know what you mean." His fist hit the table. "You wish I'd never come. I'm not good enough for your rich friends."

She forced her face to soften a bit. "It's not that, Lucky. I haven't seen Hank in years, yet he's been good enough to allow me to stay in his home and even offered to help me get Gram's house ready. If it weren't for him——"

"If it weren't for him, I'd have probably heard from you more often."

She didn't like the accusing tone of his voice. She'd called him as often as she could.

"That's one reason I came on ahead. I didn't like the way you'd always cut me off on the phone when that guy came into the room. I had a feeling you hadn't told him about me, and I'd like to know why." His voice was loud and brash. "I am your boyfriend, or have you forgotten?"

She put a finger to her lips. "Remember, Lucky, we're not alone. Faynola is in the kitchen. I don't want her to overhear us. You know she'll go right to Hank with our words."

"So? Let her! What're we sayin' old Hank shouldn't hear?"

Tina clenched her fists. "Let's just let it drop. Okay?" She stood to her feet and began gathering up their plates.

"Whatcha doin' that for? Let that maid do it!"

Angry at his words, she snatched the napkin out from beneath his elbow, nearly tipping over his beer. "She is not a maid. She's a housekeeper."

"Same thing in my book. She's gettin' paid to do that kind of stuff."

"But not for two additional people! I certainly don't expect her to wait on me, and neither should you." She spun around and headed for the kitchen.

"Aren't we gonna have cake or pie?" he called after her.

"You defy Hank's wishes, and then you have the nerve to ask about dessert? Look! Either I'm not making myself clear, or you're just plain stupid! No beer in Hank's house! I mean that, Lucky. If you can't abide by the rules, you're out of here!"

Lucky lifted his palms toward her. "Okay! Okay! I hear ya."

"Good! Because that's the way it's going to be. None of that stuff on the Gordon premises! Ever!"

He nodded, then began to rummage around in his right pocket, then the left. "Got any money, Tina? I'm a bit short."

She glared at him, her patience with him nearly exhausted.

"Did you quit your job again?"

"Not exactly."

"What's that mean? You were working at the garage and getting paid pretty good for someone with no experience as a mechanic. What happened?"

Lucky's fingers stroked at his untamed beard. "I sorta got fired."

"Fired? You got fired? Again? Do you realize how long I had to talk to convince that man to hire you? How could you? After I'd worked so hard to help you find that job."

"He accused me of stealing."

"Did you steal from him?"

"Not exactly."

"How could you not exactly steal? Either you did, or you didn't!"

"I only borrowed a few of his old tools. If he'd needed them I'd-a brought them back. I'm sure his insurance would've replaced them."

Tina couldn't believe what she was hearing. Glen Coven had been kind enough to give Lucky a chance, and this is the way he repaid him—by stealing his tools!

"Besides, the work was too hard. That man expected me to crawl under those trucks and lay on my back on that creeper thing. My arms got tired, havin' to reach up all day."

"Other men do hard work like that. I'd think a body builder who spends as much time at the gym as you do could handle it with no trouble at all. If he wanted to work. That's your problem, Lucky. You don't want to work!"

"Sure I do. I'm gonna find me a job here in Juneau, right after I help you get that house ready for your grandma."

"Good, I'm glad to hear it, but I really don't need your help on the house. I think it'd be best if you go ahead and get you a job now. I'm running low on funds. I won't be able to give you money much longer."

Lucky groaned. "Aw, Tina. I need a break. I'll get a job later."

"No, you'd better get it now. I'm going to ask Hank to help you find a job. He seems to know everyone in Juneau."

"Is it all right if I finish clearing the table, Miss Tina?"

Tina whirled around to find Faynola standing behind her and wondered just how much she'd heard. Probably most of it. "Fine," she said, her voice changing quickly from one of anger to appreciation. "We're finished, and the dinner was delicious. Thank you."

"Yeah, Fantasia," Lucky inserted, "it wasn't half bad."

The two stood silently as Faynola placed the things on her tray. "May I get you anything else?"

"I was just tellin' Tina, I could sure go for a big piece of pie. Got any?"

"Lucky!"

Faynola gave the man a gentle smile. "As a matter of fact, I baked an apple pie this afternoon. It's Mr. Gordon's favorite. I was going to wait until he got home to cut it."

Tina could almost see Lucky's mouth watering.

"Well, cut it now!" he told the woman as he grabbed her arm and nearly dragged her toward the kitchen. "Got any ice cream to go with it?"

Tina stood aghast at his rude behavior. She had to get him out of Hank's home as fast as she could. If she could get Lucky to help her, maybe she could get the house ready to have the carpet laid sooner than expected. *Dreamer. Lucky has only one speed when it comes to work. Slow!*

"Miss Tina, may I offer you a slice?" Faynola asked, as she placed a large wedge of pie on a plate, topped it with two generous scoops of ice cream, and handed it to the man.

"Thank you, Faynola," she answered, narrowing her eyes and shaking her head with disgust at Lucky, who'd already begun to devour the pie. "I think I'll wait and have mine when Hank gets home. I want to hear all about the banquet."

For some reason, Lucky's loud chewing and bad manners were really getting to her. Was it because she'd been away from him for several weeks? Those things had bothered her before, but nothing like they did now. Could it be because she'd been spending so much time with Hank? A real gentleman? Or was Lucky deliberately trying to annoy her?

She watched as Faynola busied herself at the sink, rinsing dishes and loading them into the dishwasher. Tina knew the woman felt uncomfortable hearing their bantering and let the subject drop. "Well, I've got some paperwork to do. I'm going to my room," she told them with a yawn. "Let me know when Hank gets home."

"Maybe you can take a short nap so you'll be all rested up for Peter Pan when he gets back," Lucky said with a snarl, chomping on his last bite of pie. He turned to Faynola, who was still working at the sink, her back to him. "Hey, Farina, did you know Tina and Peter Pan was sweet on each other when they was kids?"

"That's not true!" Tina shouted at the man, her patience wearing thin. "He was my best friend! That's all!"

Faynola stared at the two of them. "Who is Peter Pan?"

"Hank," Lucky answered simply, with a devious grin.

Tina moved toward him angrily, accidentally knocking over the can.

"Now see what you've gone and done!" He jumped to his feet, brushing the splatters of beer from his leather vest with the palms of his hand. "I hope you're proud of yourself, Miss High and Mighty!"

Faynola hurriedly handed a dish towel to Lucky, then began dropping more towels onto the table and the floor, before bending to blot up the spills.

"No," Tina told her, stooping down beside her and taking the wet towels from her hands, "I'll do it. It was my fault. Let me clean it up."

"I don't—"

"I know you don't mind, Faynola, but you work too hard as it is. You're not going to clean up my messes."

"What a waste of good beer," Lucky said, blotting at his wet clothing, "and look what you've done to my vest!"

Tina couldn't remember a time she'd been more furious. The stench of the spilled beer was nearly making her sick to her stomach. But she bit her tongue and kept control of the comment that nearly forced its way out of her mouth. "It'll dry," she said, willing herself to sound calm.

They all turned as the outside door opened and in stepped Hank.

Hank stared at the three of them. Tina on her hands and knees wiping up the floor. Lucky with stains on his leather vest. And Faynola looking as if she'd seen a ghost. "What's going on here?"

"Not much, Hank Old Boy," Lucky explained in an almost jovial manner. "Little spill, that's all. Tina did it."

Hank frowned as he stooped and took the wet towels from Tina's hands. "Looks more like a flood, I'd say."

"I'm so sorry, Mr. Gordon." Faynola took the towels from her employer. "It was all my fault."

Tina stood quickly to her feet. "I'm the one who knocked that can off the table, not you."

Hank stepped in and positioned himself between the three. "Look, I don't care whose fault it was. That beer should not have been in this house in the first place!"

He turned toward Lucky, angry and frustrated with the man. "I thought I'd made myself clear. I don't want that stuff anywhere around, and I'd better not find it here again! I mean it! Got it?"

Lucky gave him a smirk and turned away.

Hank gave him an I-mean-business look. "Let's just drop it."

Without turning back, Lucky gave him a grunt.

Restraining himself, Hank turned to Faynola. "Get me that yellow plastic bucket from the garage, and I'll clean this floor up for you. You have no business getting down on your knees with your arthritis. Tina, take those wet towels into the laundry room and start the washer. You'll find the detergent on the shelf." He turned to face Lucky. "It's late, and you've been up since dawn. Why don't you take you a nice hot shower and go on to bed? I'm sure Tina wants to get an early start on her grandmother's house tomorrow, and she could sure use your help. It's been a long day for all of us. You ladies go on to bed. I'll finish up here and turn out the lights."

After saying a quick good night, the women moved in the direction they'd been told.

Lucky hiked up his pants and stood his ground. "Tryin' to get rid of me, huh?"

Hank gave the man a blank stare. "Get rid of you? Is there some reason I should get rid of you?"

"Me gettin' here kinda messed up your playhouse, didn't it?"

Hank frowned. "Look, Lucky. You and I don't seem to speak the same language. You'll have to explain yourself."

"You think I don't know what's been going on since Tina got here? With you two livin' here in this house."

"I don't know what you think has been going on, but believe me, nothing has. Tina is a beautiful woman, and I enjoy her company, but—"

Lucky harrumphed. "You don't expect me to believe that, do you? I know what goes on in a man's mind when he's with a purty woman, and it sure ain't friendship."

"Look," Hank said evenly, trying to control his emotions, "you don't know me, but you do know Tina. She wouldn't even consider staying at my house until she found out my housekeeper lived here full-time."

"So you're tellin' me you never even tried to come on to Tina?"

For the first time in his life, other than the day Trapper had carried his bride away, Hank wanted to bust someone in the nose. He drew in a deep breath and clenched his fists at his sides, willing them to stay there. "That's exactly what I'm telling you. I'd never put Tina in a compromising position."

"What's the matter with you?"

"Nothing's the matter with me." Hank stood up straight and tall, nose to nose with the man who seemed to bring out the worst in him. "I'm a man who loves God and respects women, and I'm proud of it."

Lucky stepped back and stared at him.

Hank drew in a deep breath and sent up a quick prayer for help. "I need to make you understand a few things. I'm a born-again Christian, which means I've confessed my sins and accepted Jesus Christ as my Savior, and—"

"You?" Lucky gave him a sardonic grin. "Mr. Goody-goody Hank Gordon, a sinner? Ya wouldn't kid me now, would ya? I can't imagine you doin' nothin' that'd be called sin. Ain't you always been a Sunday school boy? I'll bet them teachers just loved you. You was so good."

Hank struggled to keep his cool. "Yes, I was—and am—a sinner. We're all sinners. Mere mortals. I'm a sinner saved by God's grace."

Lucky gave him a puzzled look. "Whatcha mean? Was and am? I thought you was perfect."

"No, far from perfect, but I try to follow the standards God has set in His Word. But even at that, I sin. Pretty often, despite my desire to live for Him. But I go to Him in prayer daily and ask Him to forgive me. He's promised in His Word He will."

"Like how do you sin? Ya don't drink beer. Ya don't swear. Ya don't rob banks!" His face took on that same sardonic smile. "And ya claim ya ain't been tryin' to make claims on my woman. What do you do to sin?"

"Well, those things you mentioned are sins, but there are other sins too. The kind of sins folks do every day. Anger, lying, cheating, impatience, selfishness, that sort of thing. But the greatest sin of all is turning your back on God. Refusing to believe He is God and letting Him rule and reign in your life. Constantly seeking His will."

"That don't sound like much fun! Who'd want to be a Christian if you gotta live a dull life like that? Sounds to me bein' one of them so-called Christians is for sissies. Not red-blooded men like me! I kinda like bein' a sinner."

"Well, that's a decision each person has to make for themselves. But hear me, Lucky. If you ever want to talk about it,

I'm here. Nothing would make me happier than to open God's Word and share it with you."

"Well, I'll just keep that in mind. But don't hold your breath till I get there."

Hank leaned toward Lucky and zeroed in close. "One more thing. I told you absolutely no beer in this house. I don't know where you got those cans or if you have any more. But if you do, I'd suggest you immediately put it in the trash container out in the garage. I will not—I repeat—I will not have it in my home. Is that clear? If I ever find you have brought beer into this house again, I'll have to ask you to leave." He grabbed the man's wrist and leaned even closer. "Maybe you think because I'm a Christian I'll let you get by with it again. But believe me I won't. It's because I am a Christian that I'm being so firm about this."

Lucky pulled away from his grasp and rubbed at his wrist. "Okay, Man. Okay. You don't have to get so all-fired mean about it. I hear ya!"

෴

"I started the washer, Hank," Tina said as she came rushing back into the room.

"I'd better go help Faynola find the bucket." Hank disappeared into the mudroom, leaving the two of them in the kitchen.

"I'm sorry for losing my temper," Tina began, "but you simply cannot talk about Hank that way. He's a good man."

"Good for what? Makin' advances on my woman when I'm not around?"

She let out a sigh. It'd been a wearing day, and her energy had been all spent. "Let's get something straight right now. I am not your woman. I don't belong to anyone."

"You belong to me, or have you forgotten?"

His possessive words skyrocketed her anger to the overflow level. "No, I haven't forgotten! I owe you, Lucky, but you do not own me. There's a big difference."

"You mean because I haven't put a ring on your finger?"

"No, a ring has nothing to do with it. I'll never be owned by anyone. Ownership means control, and I'll never be controlled. I'm a human being. I know I've gotten far away from God, but I well remember the things I learned in Sunday school and church. I'm as important to God as anyone who has lived, lives now, or ever will live."

"I thought the man upstairs said men were more important than women—that you females were supposed to obey us males." He finished his statement with a haughty laugh that set her teeth on edge. "That man knew what he was talkin' about. If that woman hadn't disobeyed her husband in the garden, all us men'd be livin' on easy street, eatin' grapes and wearin' palm leaves."

Despite her anger, Tina had to laugh inwardly at Lucky's warped knowledge of the Scripture. "She didn't disobey her husband, Lucky. She disobeyed God. And by the way, it wasn't palm leaves, it was fig leaves, and we don't even know that for sure."

"You two discussing the Bible?" Hank asked with a perplexed look as he came in with the yellow bucket and began to fill it at the sink.

"Oh, yeah. Talkin' about the Bible is one of my favorite pastimes, right, Tina?"

The smile left her face. "I'm going to bed." With that, she turned and left the two men alone.

Lucky let out a big yawn and stretched his arms open wide. "Me too. I sure hope Farina makes a big breakfast. I'm—"

"Not tomorrow," Hank told him as he lifted the bucket from the sink and lowered it to the floor, before stooping down beside it. "Her knees have been bothering her. I think it's the change in weather. I told her to sleep in. She has a doctor's appointment tomorrow afternoon. There are a number of dry cereals in the cabinet, fresh milk and juice in the refrigerator, and a few bagels into the bread keeper. We're all on our own in the morning. I'm going in the office about six to get some extra work done. I'll probably be out of here long before the two of you are up. Help yourself to whatever you need."

Lucky listened but appeared not to comprehend what Hank was telling him. "You mean we gotta fix our own breakfast?"

"If you want to eat," Hank replied as he wrung out a rag and began mopping up the floor with a circular motion. "Or maybe you can talk Tina into cooking something for you, but don't count on that either. She usually goes by to see her grandmother before going to the house. I doubt she'll be interested in doing any cooking before she goes."

Tina came into the kitchen, wearing no makeup and dressed in her pajamas and robe. "I forgot a glass of water," she told them as she went to the cupboard, pulled out a glass, and filled it at the sink.

Lucky puckered up his face. "Old Hank says Farina can't cook breakfast in the mornin'. Her knees hurt. You gonna cook for me?"

She gave him a vacant stare. "Lucky, didn't you tell me one time you used to work at a lunch counter? As a fry cook?"

He nodded. "Yeah, a long time ago, but I never liked it."

"Well, if you're hungry in the morning, I suggest you pull out your culinary skills and cook your own breakfast. But you'd better do it early because you're going to have to not only cook your own breakfast, you're going to have to clean up after yourself. We're not going off and leaving a mess for Faynola."

"But you used to cook for me sometimes," he told her, with puppy dog eyes, "when we was livin' in Chicago."

"That was when circumstances prevented you from taking care of yourself. If you want a simple glass of juice, a cup of coffee, and a bowl of cereal, I'll be happy to pour the juice for you and put your glass, cup, bowl, and spoon in the dishwasher when you're finished, but more than that, you're on your own. But whatever you do, you'll have to do it early. I'm always out of here by seven-thirty at the latest." She turned to go but he caught her arm.

Hank wanted to add his two cents' worth, but kept quiet as

he watched, proud of Tina for making a stand and refusing to cater to the man's whims.

"How you gonna get there? Hank's leavin' early to go to his office, so he can't take us."

"He's letting me drive his pickup truck."

Lucky gestured toward Hank. "Oh? You give her some old wreck to drive while you tool around town in that flashy SUV? Some guy you are!"

Tina gave him an incredulous glare. "For your information, the pickup I'm driving is less than six months old, and it's nearly as flashy as the SUV!"

"You're trying to tell me this man lets you live in his house, eat his food, drive his new pickup, and he helps you with the remodeling—all because he's a good guy?"

"Yes, exactly."

"Or is it because you let him—"

Tina turned and walked away before he could finish his sentence.

six

It was seven-twenty when Lucky staggered into the kitchen the next morning, his long, dark hair a tangled mess, lines etched into his face. "You mean Farina's really not gonna fix breakfast?"

"Faynola is an old woman. Did you forget what Hank said about her knees? You've got ten minutes. The coffee is hot, and you can stick a bagel in the toaster to take with you."

"How come you're bein' so mean to me?"

She lowered the paper she was reading a bit more and peered at him, her eyes squinted, and she frowned. "Because you're acting like a spoiled child, that's why! To think you brought that beer in the house after Hank had warned you about it! That really upsets me!"

"I'll bet old Hankie boy isn't as innocent as he lets on. Come on, tell me the truth." Lucky's eyes narrowed as he leaned toward her. "You and I both know there's more goin' on between you two."

Her chin jutted out. "I can't believe you'd say such a thing! Don't you know me better than that?"

"I know you ain't let me do more'n kiss you!"

She pointed to her left hand. "I don't intend to let anyone do more than kiss me until there's a ring on my finger."

His tone mellowed. "Aw, Baby, I said I'd get you a ring."

"With what, Lucky? You still owe a bundle on your Harley. You were living with a buddy because your landlord threw you out, and—"

"I tried to get you to let me move in with you so—"

"I may have wandered far from God, but I still have principles. I refuse to let any man move in with me! For any reason—until I'm wearing a wedding ring!"

"You know it's that Hank guy's fault. He bugs me, him and that mangy dog of his, and he's messin' with your head, and you don't even know it."

"Messing with my head? What's that supposed to mean?"

Lucky ripped open the bread wrapper and stuck two pieces of whole wheat bread in the toaster. "You live here in this fine house for a few weeks, and you forget all about our life in Chicago. Don't you miss all the places we used to go together? The good times we used to have?"

She shook her head sadly as she folded the newspaper in half and placed it on the empty chair beside her with a grunt, still wearing a scowl. "You mean going to the midnight movie because the tickets were cheaper then and taking our own popcorn because we couldn't afford the theater's prices? Or do you mean going to those motorcycle rallies? Getting hit on by a bunch of rowdy drunks? Or maybe visiting your cousin at the local jail? Yeah, those were fun times all right."

"You sure had me fooled. I thought you liked doing those things with me," he shot back, his voice loud and accusing as he yanked open the refrigerator door.

"I never did like those things, Lucky." Realizing their voices were getting louder with each come-back, she took a deep breath before continuing, her voice an almost whisper. "I only did them because of you. Because of what you—"

He put up a hand. "You don't have to remind me."

"Two minutes," Tina said in a controlled manner, wanting to put an end to their exchange of words and looking at the wall clock. "The pickup is leaving in two minutes. You'd better get a hurry on, or you'll get left behind." She stood to her feet and picked up her cup and spoon.

Fifteen minutes later, they entered the house on Ocean View Boulevard.

⁊⦵

Hank had a hard time keeping his mind on his work. After much persuasion, when he'd phoned Faynola, she'd reluctantly filled him in on the tense conversation she'd overheard between Tina and Lucky.

Why? Hank asked himself over and over. *Why would Tink put up with the man? How could she put up with him? None of it makes any sense. Not only is Lucky not Tina's type, he's downright rude! Surely Tink's tastes and standards haven't lowered that much since she left Juneau. But—she has been living in Chicago all this time, and from the sounds of it, in a not-too-nice neighborhood. Perhaps she's gotten used to having men like Lucky around her all the time. She said she hadn't gone to church in years, which is where she should have been if she wanted to find a good, solid man who loves God.*

He shuffled a few papers on his desk and stacked them up neatly, barely aware of what he was doing. Maybe she wasn't interested in a good, solid man who loved God. The thought made him shudder. If only she'd talk to him about Lucky, explain what she saw in the man. He glanced at the sleek chrome desk clock one of his grateful clients had given him when he'd won a difficult case. Ten o'clock.

He picked up the phone and dialed, hoping Lucky wouldn't be the one to answer. He had to talk to her. To make sure she was okay. He was concerned about her being alone with that man, although why it concerned him, he didn't know. No telling how many times she'd been alone with that character when they were in Chicago. Still, she was in Juneau now, and he felt the need to protect her.

He became more concerned with each ring, finally hanging up after he'd counted to twelve. Next he phoned Faynola.

"No, Mr. Gordon. I haven't heard a word from them. Like I told you when you called, they left about seven-thirty."

He thanked Faynola after asking her to let him know if they returned home, then stared at the phone. Where could they be? Next he phoned the nursing home, but they hadn't been there. Surely they hadn't gone to the lumberyard. He'd made sure they had all the supplies they'd be needing for their current projects.

He jumped when his secretary entered the room, his mind

on the people who should be at the house on Ocean View Boulevard.

"Sorry to interrupt, Hank," she told him as she placed a call slip on his desk. "Jean Carter just phoned. Her car won't start. She won't be able to make her ten-thirty appointment."

Hank stood quickly to his feet with a smile. "No problem. I need to be away for a couple of hours anyway."

The woman's eyes rounded, and she seemed surprised by his words. "But what about that brief you wanted me to type up for you? I thought you were in a hurry to get it—"

Hank patted her shoulder as he grabbed his coat from the rack and raced past her. "I'll have it for you sometime this afternoon."

On the way to Tina's house, he redialed her number on his cell phone. Still no answer.

❧

Tina frowned at Lucky. "The least you could do is help me with this. You're taller than I am. It'd be easier for you to reach. I've already done most of the others."

Lucky shook his head. "I think it's better if I hold onto the ladder for you, to steady it."

Tina shrugged. "Whatever."

"I don't know why you wanna wash those stupid windows anyway. It's cold out here."

She squeezed the trigger on the bottle of window cleaner before pulling a fresh rag from her jacket pocket. "I know, but this is the first time the sun has been shining all week. I wanted to take advantage of its warmth on the glass." She ran the rag in a circular motion over the window pane until it sparkled before starting back down the ladder.

"Can we quit now?"

She sent an exasperated look toward him as her foot touched the ground. "I still have the east window to do, but I guess this is enough for today."

The sound of a car pulling into the driveway caught her attention. "Wonder who that is? Can't be Hank; it's too early for him to come by on his lunch hour."

"Why haven't you been answering your phone?" Hank yelled out as he rounded the corner of the house and rushed toward them. "I've been calling for nearly an hour."

She gave him a puzzled look as she gestured toward the clean windows. "I've been up there on the ladder. I wanted to take advantage of the sunshine."

"You could have let me know!"

She let out a chuckle as her eyes filled with mock amusement. "Let you know that I was going outside to wash windows? Whatever for?"

"Yeah," Lucky chimed in with a deriding smirk. "Who do you think you are? Her keeper?"

Hank blushed and fumbled for words. "Ah, no—it's just— well, when I—the phone rang—"

Tina's gloved hand reached out and patted his cheek. "Thanks, Hank, for being concerned about me, but—"

"But she don't need you. I'm here to take care of her," Lucky inserted quickly, stepping between the pair, standing with the toes of their shoes nearly touching.

What's with these guys? Tina lifted her hands in despair. "What is this? You two haven't said a pleasant word to each other since—"

"He always starts it!" Lucky's finger shot out accusingly.

"I do not," Hank responded defensively.

"Whoa! Enough." Tina stomped her foot and tugged at each grown man's sleeve. "I feel like I'm back in the third grade, with you two bantering like this." She turned to Lucky and ordered, "Go into the house and start sanding on that back bedroom door."

Lucky gave her an unpleasant snort but did as she'd instructed, grumbling beneath his breath all the way to the back door.

Once he was out of sight and she heard the door slam, she turned to Hank, both hands on her hips. "Now for you! What's with you, Hank? I know it's asking a lot of you to let

Lucky and me both stay at your house, but you're the one who invited us. I would never—"

"Surely you know I only invited him because of you. I didn't want you to leave! I like having you stay at my house."

"I–I like being there too."

Hank stepped forward and took her hands in his. "Why Lucky, Tink?"

She looked away, avoiding his kind eyes. "I don't know what you mean."

His forefinger slipped beneath her chin, tilting her head upward, causing her to face him. "He's not the man for you. I think we both know that, but for the life of me, I can't figure out what kind of hold he has on you. I know you don't love—"

"Could—could we talk about this later?"

"Hey," Lucky called loudly, as he stood holding the back door open. "Keep your hands off my woman!"

Tina backed quickly away from Hank and headed toward the house. "Are you coming in?"

"No, guess not. I'd better get back to the office if I'm going to be able to get away at five and come and help you. Or maybe with Lucky here, you don't need me."

Tina turned around slowly. "Oh, Hank, Lucky could never take your place."

He grinned shyly. "That's what I was hoping."

"And besides, I think he's starting that new job tomorrow at a car wash."

❧

Hank moved toward the bed with a smile. "Hi, Mrs. Taylor. How are you feeling this morning?"

Harriett Taylor reached out a trembling hand. "Oh, Hank. Come and sit by me. These old eyes of mine can't see you very well."

He pulled up a chair and sat down, taking her frail hand in his. It seemed to him she was even more fragile than she'd been the last time he'd visited her. "Tina's coming by later. I haven't seen you for a day or two. I hope you aren't too disappointed it's just me."

"I'm probably the envy of all the ladies here at the nursing home, having a handsome man come to visit me. Of course I'm not disappointed. You've always been very special to me."

"Tina's really working hard on your house. You should see the things she's getting done. In no time at all she'll be able to take you home."

She gave him a little smile. "From what my granddaughter tells me, you're doing a lot of the work. How can I ever thank you?"

"By taking care of yourself. That's all."

Her face became serious. "I'm so glad you're spending time with Tina. I don't like that Lucky fellow. I try to stay out of her business. But when you're as old as I am, and you love someone, it's hard to keep quiet."

He patted her hand. "All we can really do, Mrs. Taylor, is pray."

"I'm praying she'll forget all about that awful man and start paying more attention to you."

He weighed his words carefully before answering, finally saying, "Me too."

❧

The next evening, Hank showed up at Tina's at exactly five-thirty, his arms loaded with carryout food, which Lucky began to devour the moment he came in the door. Lucky started eating even before Hank had time to thank the Lord, and afterward parked himself on a kitchen chair and watched television on the little set her grandmother had kept, while Tina and Hank worked on the house.

"Well, that's it," Tina said with a smile, as she brushed her palms together. "I think we're finally ready for the carpet installation."

Hank stood back and admired their work. "Yep, soon as they get that carpet down I'll nail the baseboards in place, and you'll be ready for the furniture."

She stood on tiptoe and kissed his cheek. "Only because of

you. I could never have done this without you. Gram will be so pleased. I told her we were nearly finished."

Hank looked over her shoulder through the kitchen door and, seeing Lucky engrossed in a movie, seized the opportunity and threw his arms about Tina, pulling her to him and kissing her sweet mouth. He'd longed to kiss her since the day she'd come back into his life. He was surprised when she didn't struggle to free herself. "Oh, Tink," he said softly into her ear when he finally, reluctantly, ended their kiss. "Do you have any idea how much I've wanted to kiss you?"

"I–I—"

His lips sought hers again, cutting off her words. This time he felt her arms circle his neck as she leaned into him and kissed him back. "Hank, oh, Hank."

"Hey, Tina, bring me some of those peanut butter cookies!" Lucky called out when a commercial blared from the TV.

Hank propelled himself quickly past Tina and into the kitchen. "She's not your servant, Lucky! That woman has been working hard all day." Hank paused. "If you were half a man, you'd be doing the heavy work instead of watching her do it!"

The look on Lucky's face as he jumped to his feet should've prepared Hank for what was to come, but it didn't. He was not at all ready for the blow of the man's fist on his chin and the blood that gushed forth from his lip.

Tina sprang forward and set herself up as a barricade between them, screaming for Lucky to stop. But Lucky only pushed her aside and followed up with a second blow that hit Hank squarely in the gut, knocking the wind out of him and leaving him gasping for air.

Instinctively, Hank's survival mechanism kicked into gear. He sucked in a deep breath, clenched his fists, and plowed into Lucky, hitting him first on the cheek, then the shoulder, then the stomach.

Lucky reeled a bit, seemed to regroup, then doubled up a fist and struck out again, this time landing it on Tina as she once again stepped in between them, his ring biting into her face.

She screamed and fell backward into Hank's arms, blood running down her cheek and flowing onto her sweatshirt.

"Look what you've done to her!"

"Your fault as much as mine," Lucky retorted angrily. "I thought you Christians were supposed to turn the other cheek."

"Is that what you were counting on?" Hank snapped back as he glared at the man. "Hurry up! Get one of those new dish towels out of that drawer next to the sink. Wet it down with cool water, wring it out, and bring it to me. Now!" Hank ordered as he protectively pulled Tina close, not about to let the repulsive man get an inch nearer to his precious Tink. "Hurry up! I'm taking her to the hospital. This cheek'll probably need stitches, thanks to you!"

"I'll take her. She's my—"

"What are you going to pay the hospital with? Empty beer cans?" After pressing the wet towel to Tina's cheek, Hank scooped her up in his arms and headed for the door. "Do you think you can turn off the lights and lock up? Or is that asking too much?"

Lucky shrugged. "Okay, you take her."

Hank pushed past the man without so much as a look back, his only concern for Tina.

As he glanced at the shaking woman sitting in the SUV, so close beside him, her head resting on his shoulder, her shirt soaked with blood, a cold wet towel pressed to her cheek, love for her filled his heart. Surely this episode would cause Tina to see Lucky for what he was. A loser. A real loser.

"Hank."

"Yes."

"Don't be mad at Lucky. You don't know him like I do. He's not as bad as he seems."

Hank slipped an arm about her shoulders and kissed the top of her head. "He's not the man for you, Tink."

"I don't have any choice. I have to marry Lucky," she whispered softly as she pressed the towel to her face.

Hank stiffened at her words. "You're not—"

seven

"Pregnant? No!" Tina said emphatically, pulling away slightly and lifting her face to his with a groan. "How could you ask me such a thing?"

"Look, Tink, I'm sorry to have even considered something like that, but for the life of me I can't think of one good reason you'd even consider marrying that man!"

"I wish you hadn't hit him."

"Me hit him? He started it. What was I supposed to do? Stand there and let him use me as a punching bag?" A faint smile curled at his lips as he remembered his fracas with Lucky, totally amazed by how quickly things had happened and how he'd automatically responded. He'd never hit another man in his entire life. Not even Trapper when he'd taken Glorianna from him on his wedding day. Yet he'd held his own with Lucky. His lip and chin were sore, and his stomach felt like he'd run into a brick wall. But other than that, and a few feelings of guilt, he felt fine.

"Maybe it'd be best if Lucky and I moved out of your house. We could—"

"No! I won't hear of it." The idea made Hank ill. If Tina moved out he wouldn't have an excuse to be around her, not with her allegiance to Lucky. He couldn't let that happen. Not yet, anyway. And he certainly didn't want them staying in Harriett Taylor's house alone. "You two better stay in my home until the carpet is laid and the furniture delivered."

When they arrived at the hospital, Hank parked next to the emergency room door, disregarding the no parking sign. As he'd suspected, the cheek required stitches, but only two small ones. He cringed and felt the pain right along with her as he watched the doctor work the curved needle through her delicate skin, feeling guilty and knowing he was partially responsible for her injury.

Two hours later, after he'd made sure Tina was resting comfortably, he knelt beside his bed, unsure what to say to God. After thanking Him for all the blessings He'd bestowed upon him by bringing Tina back into his life, he decided it was time to get serious. *Lord, I've actually had a fistfight,* he confessed. *Me. Hank Gordon. The man who has always abhorred violence of any kind. I've let that man bring out the worst in me and I'm not very proud of it!*

He gulped hard, then continued. "God," he asked aloud this time, with a glance upward as he let out a deep sigh. "Was Lucky right? Was I, as a Christian, supposed to turn my cheek after he'd hit me and let him use it as a target? Is that really what you meant in Your Word?"

He waited, but no answer came from heaven. No thunderbolts jagged their way to earth. No lightning ripped across the sky. But in his heart, Hank was sure his Lord understood why he'd done what he'd done.

Since there were no sounds of stirring in either Tina's or Lucky's room the next morning, Hank decided to forgo breakfast at home and instructed Faynola to let them sleep in and not awaken them early, as Tina had requested. She'd been sure she'd feel like working at the house that day, but Hank knew better and had advised her to take the day off and spend it with her grandmother, resting and recouping from her injury.

He wheeled into the convenience store parking lot, selected two raised doughnuts and a cup of coffee from the deli section, and proceeded to the cash register.

"That'll be two-seventy-seven," the clerk told him.

Hank reached into his pocket for his billfold, only to find it empty. He was sure when he'd bought gas there had still been two twenty-dollar bills left in that billfold. He fumbled around in his pocket for change and, by using a combination of quarters, dimes, nickels and two pennies, came up with the amount. *I know I had two twenties,* he reasoned to himself as he climbed into the SUV and headed for his office.

He phoned home at ten. "How is Tina?" he asked when Faynola answered on the first ring.

"I looked in on her a bit ago. She's still sleeping," the old woman whispered into the phone. "But that man is gone. He left in your pickup about an hour ago."

Hank frowned. "Lucky has my pickup? Was he driving it to the car wash and leaving Tina stranded there without transportation?"

"Sorry, Mr. Gordon. He didn't say. Just told me to fix him some sausage, eggs, and pancakes, ate them, and left."

"He told you to fix him breakfast?"

"Yes, Sir, and—"

"Faynola, you do not have to take orders from that man. Don't let him walk all over you like that!"

"But he's your guest. I would never—"

"He's only a guest because of Tina. I do not want you going out of your way for him. I mean that, Faynola! I'm your boss, not Lucky. You do what I say!"

The phone was silent for a moment, and Hank thought perhaps the connection had failed or he'd upset her with his strong words.

"I—" Silence again. "I hate to have to tell you this, but last night, when I got up about four o'clock to get a drink of water, I saw Mr. Wheeler standing by the front hall table. I wondered what he was doing up at that time, so I watched him. He was taking some money out of a billfold. You'd left your billfold on that table."

Hank could feel his blood pressure rising. *That explains the missing twenties.* "I'll take care of it, Faynola. Thanks for telling me, but I doubt he was taking money out of my billfold. Just keep an eye on Tina for me, please. And don't say anything to her about this. I don't want to upset her."

"Mr. Gordon, that's not all."

"Oh no. There's more? Why am I not surprised? What else?"

"After I saw him take the money out of the billfold, I kept an eye on him. He--he went into your office. I don't know what he was doing in there. I'd planned to tell you this first thing this morning, but you left much earlier than I'd expected."

Hank couldn't remember a time he'd been so angry, but he kept his voice as even as possible. "Did he see you?"

"No, Sir."

"Thank you, Faynola. I'll take care of it, and remember, not a word about this to Tina."

Struggling to keep his anger at bay, Hank glanced at his bruised fist, then dialed Tina's phone number at the house, thinking maybe Lucky was there. But even after waiting while the phone rang twenty-three times, no one answered. He no longer had to wonder what had happened to the missing forty dollars, but where was Lucky? Or more importantly, where was the truck? And if he'd found his lockbox in the office, how much more money had the man taken?

At eleven Hank drove by Tina's house, and seeing no truck in the drive, headed on home. Tina was sitting at the kitchen table watching Faynola peel carrots for their evening meal and gave him a lopsided smile as he entered. The small bandage on her face did little to cover the blue and purplish bruise on her cheek. "You were right," she told him as he sat down beside her and folded her hand in his, "I do feel kinda lousy today. Those pain pills the doctor gave me made me drowsy. I decided to take the day off as you recommended. I called Gram, and we had a nice visit, but I never got to the nursing home."

"I'm sorry you didn't get to see Harriett, but I'm glad you're resting. You've been working way too hard. We'll see how you feel tomorrow."

"He took your truck."

"I know. Faynola told me. Do you have any idea where he was going?"

She shook her head. "No, I didn't even know he was taking it. He's asked to borrow it before, but I've never let him."

"Well," Hank said, forcing a smile, "don't worry about it.

He probably had a good reason." *Yeah, forty, and about another thousand dollars' worth of good reason, if he took everything I had in the lockbox.* "I have a feeling you've been giving him money. Have you?"

"Ah—some. But I'm beginning to reach the bottom of my savings account, so I haven't been able to give him much lately. He's really been down on his luck lately."

"Yeah, so I've heard a dozen times from him. I've tried to help the man, but he's left every job I've gotten him. Isn't it about time he started looking for one on his own? Started accepting some responsibility for himself? Maybe that's where he is now. He sure hasn't been much help on the house."

The tip of her finger idly traced the pattern on the table-cloth. "He got fired from the car wash job. He says he's been scanning the newspaper for openings, but, so far, he hasn't been interested in any of them, or they've informed him he doesn't have the necessary skills. I told him maybe if he went to apply for them in person, rather than over the phone, it might help."

Not the way he looks, with that long, dangling earring and that smart mouth of his! "Tina, from what you've told me, money has been in short supply for you. How can you just hand your hard-earned wages over to an able-bodied man like Lucky? Don't you realize you're only encouraging his laziness?"

"Please don't talk about him that way, Hank. You don't know how much he means to me."

"No, I guess I don't," he said, rising with a shake of his head. "I have a lunch appointment with a client. I only stopped by to see how you were doing." He bent and kissed her good cheek. "See you about five-thirty."

≥≥

It was nearly eight-thirty that evening before Lucky showed up with Hank's pickup. Hank had been waiting for him, but decided to confront him alone later, for Tina's sake. He'd already checked the lockbox. The man had picked the lock and taken the money. Hank fully intended to call the sheriff, but his thoughts went to Tina. Would she believe Lucky was a thief? Faynola hadn't actually seen him open the lockbox.

He waited until the man entered the house, then checked out his pickup, making sure there hadn't been any dents or damage inflicted on it since he'd last seen it. From the outside, it looked fine. But inside was another story. Empty beer cans, candy bar and chewing gum wrappers, and greasy French fries were strewn about the cab, on the seat, as well as on the floor, and the ashtray was filled with cigarette butts. The stench nearly got to Hank as he backed away and slammed the door. This would be the last time that ungrateful man took his truck. He'd see to that! He'd lent it to Tina, not Lucky, and he was going to make sure both his houseguests knew it. He only hoped Tina would understand.

❧

All day, Tina had been seething at Lucky's audacity. "Tell me where you've been!" she demanded as he sauntered into the house, as if he didn't have a care in the world.

"I'd say it's nobody's business where I've been," he snorted back angrily, as he shoved past her toward the kitchen. "I'm a grown man, or have you forgotten?"

She followed close at his heels. "It became my business when you took Hank's truck without permission."

"And there's the little question of the forty bucks missing from my wallet and a little over a thousand dollars from my lockbox!" Hank inserted irately as he came in from the garage and joined them in the wide hallway.

Lucky stopped midstride with a menacing glare, first at one and then the other. "What is this? Stack-it-on-Lucky day?"

Tina's mouth gaped. "You stole money from Hank's wallet and his lockbox? Then took his truck without permission? After all he's done for you? How dare you? You're nothing but a common thief!"

"Oh?" Lucky's brows lifted, then lowered into a frown as deep lines folded into his forehead. "You believe what that man says? How do you know he didn't make all this up to make me look bad?"

"You don't deserve this good woman," Hank said, stepping in front of Tina protectively, his face mere inches from his rival's. "You know good and well you took that money. Faynola saw you with my wallet. Are you accusing her of lying too?"

"Sure, she'd lie. She works for you, don't she?"

"But she'd never lie for me. The best thing you could do for Tina is to get lost. I'd half hoped you wouldn't show up at all. It'd be worth losing my pickup truck and the money, just to get you out of her life! I'd even treat you to a one-way airline ticket back to Chicago!"

Lucky's fist shot out again. But this time, Hank was ready for him and blocked it by grabbing the man's arm and quickly twisting it up behind his back, a defensive move he'd seen in old movies. But Lucky responded with a counter move Hank hadn't expected and sent him reeling backward into the wall, knocking two framed pictures from their moorings and sending them crashing to the floor.

"Now see what you've done!" Tina flew into Lucky, her anger soaring, her doubled-up fists crashing against his chest. "After Hank has put up with all your foolishness and even helped you get those jobs!"

"You're taking his side? Against me? I'm the man you're going to marry. Not him!" Lucky grabbed both her wrists and held her at arm's length, his eyes narrowed, his face gnarled into a threatening scowl. "He hasn't done a thing for me, Tina. It's all been for you! Don't you see? Everything that man has done has been to keep you from me! He's crazy about you!"

Tina stopped struggling and glared at him. "That's a rotten thing to say! Hank and I are just good friends, or at least we were until you pulled this trick! Now he probably hates me for bringing you into his life!" Tina yelled back at him.

Lucky looked over his shoulder at Hank. "Tell her! Be man enough to admit it!"

Hank seemed to grope for words. "If I have any feelings for Tink, I've kept them to myself, out of deference to you. Not because of anything worthwhile I've seen in you, Lucky, but because of what Tina seems to see in you. But I will admit, I do not think you are the right man for her!"

"It's really none of your business, Mr. Know-it-all! You're just jealous because she's mine!"

"I don't belong to anyone!" Tina screamed, her face belying her frustration. "Apologize to Hank now, Lucky! I mean it! And you're going to give back every cent you've stolen from him!"

"Oh, yeah? Says who?" With that, Lucky released her and headed down the hall toward his room, banging his fists into the walls as he went. "Satan will turn into a snowman before I apologize to that man!"

Hank bit back his anger, gently took Tina by the arm, and led her into the kitchen, where Faynola stood waiting, ready to spoon out the beef stew she'd prepared. "Let's forget about him for now. Okay?"

She nodded, brushing back a tear. "I'm so sorry—"

"You needn't be. It wasn't your fault."

"But it was," she said, dropping into the chair he'd pulled out from the table. "I brought him here."

The loud slamming of the front door, then the roar of Hank's truck starting, brought them both to their feet. But by the time they reached the front porch, the truck was speeding down the street, with Lucky at the wheel.

"I'm going to call the sheriff and have that man arrested!" Hank shouted, angrily shaking his fist, as he stood staring at the cloud of dust whirling up behind the pickup.

Tina grabbed his wrist, her eyes pleading. "No, please! Don't cause him any trouble. I'm sure he'll bring it back."

Hank couldn't believe what he was hearing. "Look, Tink! This man turned up unexpectedly on my doorstep and invited himself to stay in my home. He brought beer into the house against my wishes. Made more work for Faynola. Tried to assault me. Twice! Stole my money. Took my truck without asking. Not to mention how disrespectfully he treats you! And you're asking me not to call the sheriff? Come on. Get serious!"

"Please, Hank," she whispered softly as she gazed up at him, her eyes filled with tears, her tone imploring. "I'm begging you. Don't call the sheriff! You don't know the things Lucky's gone through. He's had a pretty rough life."

There was something about the way she asked him that seemed to melt his resolve, despite his anger. "He doesn't deserve you, you know! Why do you put up with that man? Do you have any idea what you're asking?"

He was disappointed when Tina ignored his question and simply repeated, "Please don't call the sheriff. For me?"

Hank allowed his face to soften some. "Okay, I won't call—this time. But I'm tired of putting up with him, Tink! You'd better keep him in line, and I want that money back. If he doesn't return it, all of it, I will call the sheriff! We can't let Lucky continue to get by with such things!"

"M–maybe I can repay you, if you'll—"

"No!" he fairly shouted at her. "Don't even think it! I want it from him!"

❧

Once they were back in the house and he was alone in his study, he phoned a lawyer friend in Chicago who worked closely with the district attorney's office. "Yeah, Lucky Wheeler," he said in a low voice to the man on the other end. "I'm almost certain the guy's got a record. See what you can find out."

eight

Despite her concern about Lucky's whereabouts, the next two days were the happiest Tina had ever spent as she and Hank put the finishing touches on the house.

"Do you think he went back to Chicago?" she asked Hank, as he placed a new log on the fire that evening. "It's been two days since he left."

"I don't know. I hope so. But that would mean he either abandoned my pickup or sold it. He sure couldn't drive it out of Juneau. My guess is that he conned one of the seaplane pilots to take him to Anchorage or Vancouver."

"I thought I knew the man so well. I feel responsible for—"

"Look, I'm not going to let him ruin our evening. Let's put Lucky out of our minds, if just for a few hours. Okay?"

Tina dropped to the floor and leaned back against the newly upholstered sofa and wrapped her arms about her legs. "What did you mean when you used the word if?"

Hank grabbed the iron poker from the hearth and stirred up the coals before sitting down beside her. "When I used the word if? When did I use it? I don't know what you mean."

"The night Lucky left. You said, 'If you had any feelings for me.' I just wondered what *if* meant. That's all."

"Oh, that word," he answered with a shy grin.

She scooted a bit closer to him, cocked her head a bit, and looked up into his eyes with an impish smile. "Yes, that word."

Hank stared into the fire for a long moment before responding to her poignant question. "Tink," he began slowly, "when you showed up in that department store that day, I–I—"

She gave a slight nudge to his ribs with her elbow. "Yes?"

"It—it was like you were a gift from God. I even thanked the Lord for sending you to me. I was so sure you were the answer to my prayers. I wouldn't admit this to anyone but you, but I've been pretty lonely these past few years. I haven't had anyone special in my life since—"

"Since Sheila—and Glorianna?"

He nodded.

"I thought maybe you and I could get together again, but when I met Lucky—"

"I guess you were surprised—"

"Worse than surprised, Tink. Shocked is a better word."

"I know I should have told you about him, but I honestly didn't think the two of you would ever meet. He wasn't supposed to come until after I called him. Then I met you at Beck's, moved into your house, and you began helping me, and—"

He shifted slightly to face her. "Why, Tink? Why Lucky? You two are nothing alike. How could you even consider marrying him? The man's not only obnoxious, he's a thief!"

Tina shuddered and began to weep uncontrollably. She no longer felt like smiling. "Oh, Hank, it's such a long story. I hardly know where to begin, but I–I guess I–I need to tell you the whole thing. You've been so kind, you deserve to know."

"Take your time. Begin anywhere you like."

Staring into the fire, her mind going back to that dreadful night and all of its ramifications, she began. She hated to have to repeat her awful ordeal. "I was penniless when I decided it was time to leave Juneau. I had to get away and start making it on my own. I borrowed five hundred dollars from Gram, plus enough money to get a plane ticket to Chicago, and—"

"Why Chicago? Why not Los Angeles? Or maybe Dallas?"

"Because I'd heard the jobs were plentiful in Chicago, and they paid pretty good too. I couldn't find an affordable apartment and ended up staying at the Rescue Mission for a couple of weeks. The people there were really nice. They helped me find a job and a place to live with a couple who worked second shift at a factory. They needed a baby-sitter to stay nights with their three children. In return, they gave me a place to stay and food to eat. I don't know what I would've done without them."

"Poor Tink. I never knew."

She could almost feel his compassion as his fingers entwined with hers. "I–I lived with them for nearly a year, saving every penny I could. I finally moved into a tiny apartment right next to the El, I read about the job with Beesom Parts, applied for it, and went to work in the sales department answering phones."

He nodded. "I've heard about them. Good solid company."

She smiled through her tears. "Yes, they are. And they've been good to me. From the phone job, I was promoted to the mailroom as assistant to the manager. I stayed there for about four years, taking business management courses at night at the local junior college. By the time I graduated, my company was just beginning to move its catalog onto the Internet, and I applied for a job on the design team. To my surprise, I got it. I've been there ever since, only now I'm the senior design technologist and have become part of the distribution management team."

"I'm very proud of you," Hank said, beaming with enthusiasm for her accomplishments. "It sounds like you've worked very hard to get to that position."

"I have," she agreed, wishing she could end the story there, on a high note.

"I didn't mean to interrupt. Go on with your story."

She sucked in a deep breath, knowing the rest of her tale was going to be much harder to tell. "About six years ago, after Gram fell and broke her hip, she admitted she could no longer take care of herself and needed to go into a care home. I couldn't bear the thought and invited her to leave Juneau, come to Chicago, and move in with me, so I could look after her."

"And she did?"

"Yes, but she refused to sell her house. She always said she wanted to die in her own home, like Grandpa did."

"I always liked your grandpa. Too bad he died so young."

"I know. Gram really misses him."

"So things worked out well for both of you, huh?"

She smiled. "Oh yes. Gram's been a delight to have around. We've had some great times together. She rarely complains about anything. Living together has been the best thing that could've happened to both of us."

"What did she think when you began dating Lucky?"

Her face sobered. "She never liked Lucky, but she—" Her words fell off. "Gram was always telling me I should find some nice guy and get out and enjoy life. She hated it that I spent all my free time at her side. I tried to tell her I didn't really care about dating and loved being with her, but I don't think she ever believed me. Besides, I really never met anyone I'd want to get serious with."

"Before you started dating Lucky?"

"No, Hank. It wasn't like that with Lucky and me."

Hank shrugged. "Then how was it?"

Her hand rose to cup her cheek, which was now healing nicely. "About six months ago, Gram had two bad spells with her heart. They really scared me. The second one put her in the hospital for a number of days, and her doctor said she needed someone to look after her around the clock. That's when they discovered the cancer, when they were running some routine tests on her. Her heart is terribly weak too."

"Oh, Tink, that's much like it was with Sheila. What an ordeal this has been for both of you."

"It was a real shock-a-roo all right. I located a nursing home about eight blocks from where I live and moved her there. Each night as I got off work, I'd take the El to the care home, made sure she ate her dinner, and visited with her a little bit. Sometimes we'd watch a show on TV together, and then I'd walk home."

Hank's brow lifted. "Wasn't that a little dangerous? Walking home by yourself?"

She nodded, rather than answering his question, needing time to regroup before going on. "I–I was always careful, and I tried to get home before eight. But one evening we were having so much fun, laughing and talking about Gram's childhood,

I lost track of time and it was nearly nine before I left. I decided to take the bus, but it whizzed by just as I walked out the door. Rather than wait thirty minutes for the next one, I decided to walk. I'd lived in Chicago all those years and nothing had ever happened to me. I thought I'd be fine. It was only eight blocks. I guess I'd gotten a little cocky."

She almost hoped Hank would say something, get up to add another log to the fire, make some comment that would delay her story. Anything, but he didn't. He just sat silently holding her hand.

"It was dark by the time I left. I took off down the sidewalk, looking both ways, listening for footsteps behind me, keeping an eye on anyone approaching me, but everything seemed fine. I was just two blocks from my apartment and feeling pretty confident, when I reached an alley between two tall apartment buildings. Suddenly, out of nowhere, two motorcycles came roaring down the street and turned into the alley, stopping right in front of me. I panicked. I didn't know whether to try to run around them or scream or what."

Hank's grip tightened on her hand. "You had to have been terrified!"

She took a couple of deep breaths before continuing. Just relating the events made her stomach ache. "Before I could do anything, one of the men jumped off his cycle and grabbed me and pulled me into the alley behind a Dumpster."

"What about the other man?" he prodded softly.

"He—he parked his cycle and came and stood by us, watching and laughing at me as I struggled, sneeringly flashing his knife at me. The man holding me actually told me what he was going to do to me."

"Tink! Oh, Tink! No!" Hank said with a gasp.

"I–I tried to talk him out of it, but the more I begged the tighter he held me. He smelled awful, Hank! I'll never forget that smell. Like rotting meat. I begged the other guy to help me, but he only laughed in my face and said he'd take his turn with me when his buddy got finished."

"Did they—"

"Let me go on. Hopefully then you'll understand." *This is so hard to talk about.* "I thought I was a goner. I wanted to die. If I could've gotten that man's knife away from him, I think I would have plunged it into my own heart rather than face what I knew was about to happen to me."

Pausing to look into his eyes, she saw her own fear reflected back at her. "As he pulled my coat off and ripped my blouse, I heard the sounds of another motorcycle. I was afraid it was a third man, and I was terrified! But the man on this third motorcycle was coming to my rescue. Later, I learned he'd heard me scream. Anyway, he roared right in beside us and leaped off his cycle, right on top of the man who'd ripped my blouse, and began beating on him with his fists."

Hank's eyes widened as he listened. "Not Lucky—"

"Yes, it was Lucky."

"What about the other man? The one who—"

"That man tried to pull Lucky off, but he kept right on beating the man on top of me, yelling for me to run. Finally, I succeeded in getting out from under them. I wanted to run like he'd told me, but I couldn't just leave him there, fighting off the two men alone. It was as if I was glued to the spot. I just stood and screamed, hoping someone would hear me and call the police."

"Did anyone come?"

"No. Lucky kicked the second man in the groin, and he really got mad. He stabbed that knife into Lucky's back. I watched that wretched man as he pulled it back out. There was blood all over it. Then, with his foot, he flipped Lucky over on his back and stabbed him again, this time in his stomach. I've never seen so much blood. When he lifted the knife a third time, I realized I'd better get out of there fast before they came after me."

"What did you do?"

"I ran across the street into a liquor store and asked the clerk to call the police. Then stood there in the window, trembling in fear, as I watched the first man kick Lucky in the head with the toe of his big, heavy boot before they climbed back onto their motorcycles and sped off." She went limp as her hands covered her face. "He did it for me, Hank. And he didn't even know me."

❧

Hank couldn't believe what he was hearing. Lucky, the foul, uncouth man who'd been living in his house, eating his food, taking his truck, stealing his money, using his Lord's name in vain. That Lucky had put his life on the line for a stranger? Amazing!

"He nearly died. I rode with him in the ambulance to the emergency room. The doctors and nurses on duty just shook their heads when they saw him and realized how much blood he'd lost. I even heard one of the doctors tell a nurse that Lucky wouldn't make it through the night."

"But obviously, he did," Hank replied thoughtfully, running each detail over in his mind, thinking how heroic it was for Lucky to come to Tink's rescue.

"They took him to surgery to try to repair the damage. It took almost all night. The police came to the hospital and asked all kinds of questions. The rape counselors came and questioned me, telling me how fortunate I was to have had someone come to help me like he did. I didn't even get to talk to Lucky for two days, and even then, he was too weak to respond. I learned from a friend of his, who'd seen the story on the news, that Lucky had lost his job and was without any kind of insurance, so of course I offered to pay his hospital bill."

"It must have run in the thousands, considering the surgeries and special care he probably needed!" Hank said, letting out a low whistle.

Tina let out a sigh. "It did. I'll probably be paying on it the rest of my life."

"Whew, I hadn't realized things had been that rough for you. You poor kid, I'm beginning to see why you tolerate that man."

"I'm making good money now, and I'm thankful for my job.

If it weren't for those doctor and hospital bills, I'd actually be able to live fairly comfortably."

Hank stretched his long legs out in front of him and gazed at the fire that would soon go out, if he didn't add another log. "He doesn't help with the bills?"

"No. He keeps saying he's going to, but he's been laid off a couple of times this year, and then he's had to quit a couple of jobs because of his injuries. He's not allowed to lift anything over thirty pounds. But I don't mind. I owe it to him. If it weren't for me, he'd never have been hurt like he was."

"I think I'm beginning to get the picture. You're convinced you owe that man your life, and you're willing to spend the rest of that life making it up to him, right?"

"Yes, I hadn't thought of it exactly that way, but yes, I do owe him my life. But please, don't say anything to him about this. He asked me not to tell you. He claims he's not a hero."

No, he'd rather I'd think you were madly in love with him! Hank stood to his feet, pulled a new log from the bin, and added it to the smoldering fire. "When did you decide to marry him, Tink?"

She looked up at him with such sad eyes he wanted to grab her and kiss her, to make all the hurts go away.

"It was his idea. I haven't exactly said yes."

"But you must have implied it." He hoped the disappointment in his heart wasn't revealed in his voice.

"I've never actually told him I was going to marry him, not really," she murmured softly. "I–I don't love him, not like I think a wife should love the man she's going to spend the rest of her life with."

"I knew it!" Hank said almost victoriously, slapping his palms together as he paced back and forth across the room. "I knew you didn't love him. Oh, Tink. I was so afraid—"

"But—I owe Lucky—"

He stopped pacing. "You can't marry a man you don't love. Don't you see? You'd be nothing but miserable being tied to him in that way. You'd both be miserable."

"You may be right, but I do owe him, and he wants to marry me." She covered her face with her hands, and he was sure she was crying. "I'm sorry, but this is so hard to talk about."

"And I'm sorry to put you through this, but I need to know. Make me understand." Hank could see just repeating the whole sordid experience was putting her through torture, but he had to know exactly where this fierce loyalty she had for Lucky was coming from and why she'd been willing to dedicate the rest of her life to the man.

"You don't know Lucky like I do. He can be so sweet. Sometimes, he says that—"

"Sweet?" Hank asked aloud with a grimace, stunned by her words. *Not the Lucky who followed you to Juneau! The Lucky I know seems to be taking advantage of a tragic situation, and milking it for all it's worth.* "Look, Tink," he said, trying to soften his words, when what he really wanted to do was grab her by both arms and try to shake some sense into her. The woman seemed blind where Lucky was concerned. Always ready to stand up for him and his callous ways. "I can understand your loyalty and wanting to somehow pay him back for what he did. But marriage? No! You can't do it. You can't give your entire life to him because of one good deed."

She stared at him, her brows lifted. "A good deed? It was far more than a good deed, and he needs me. He put his own life in danger for me! All of his friends talk about how much he's changed since the two of us have been together."

"I'd hate to have seen what he was like before this so-called change!" Hank said with a grunt.

"Oh, I have to admit, at first, even though I knew what would've happened to me if he hadn't come along, I was afraid of him. He—he was everything my grandmother had warned me about." She blinked hard and looked away as she swallowed at a sob. "Wh–when he came roaring into that alley, I actually thought he was those horrid men's leader."

Hank dropped back down beside her and brushed a lock of hair from her forehead. "You poor, poor baby. I can't even imagine how frightened you must've been. I didn't mean to snap at you."

"It's impossible to put into words, especially when they—"

"Shh." Hank put a finger to her lips. The pain in her voice was almost more than he could stand. For a moment he, too, felt obligated to Lucky, knowing what would've happened to his Tink if the man hadn't come along and intervened. He touched a palm to her cheek and gently lowered her head onto his shoulder. "It's okay. You're safe now. It's over."

"Sometimes, when he lets his temper get the best of him, I have to admit I'm still a bit afraid of him," Tina said, lifting her gaze to his, finally. "But I'm sure he'd never hurt me."

"Are you trying to convince me? Or yourself?" he prodded softly, as his finger touched the adhesive bandage where the doctor had placed the two tiny stitches.

"Lucky says it'd be cheaper if we were married," she went on, ignoring his question. "We'd both be staying in my apartment, instead of paying for two places."

Hank gave her a dubious look. "You'd marry the man because it's cheaper to live together? That's hardly a good reason."

"Hank! Because of his injuries it's been impossible for him to keep a job, and I can't afford to keep paying his rent too."

"You're paying his rent?" Hank couldn't believe what he was hearing. "Tink, no wonder you're having money problems! Surely the man was paying his own way before he met you! Why not now?"

"I'm sure he was, but you saw what happened when you got him those jobs here in Juneau. He had to quit the very first day because he couldn't handle the work. It was too hard for him with his physical condition, a condition he suffered coming to help me!"

"Come on, Tink, get real! Face up to it. The man lied to you! I haven't wanted to say anything about it, but I've talked to his employers. He either quit because he didn't like the work, or he got in a fight with a customer or one of the other men on the crew. His physical ability had nothing to do with it!"

She reeled back in surprise. "But he said—"

"From my vantage point, I'd say he's lied to you a number of times. Did you actually hear his doctors say he shouldn't lift over thirty pounds or do physical labor?"

"Well, no." She hung her head and fiddled with a loose thread on the hem of her shirt. "Not really. He told me that's what they'd said."

Hank shrugged and leaned back against the sofa, locking his hands behind his head. "I rest my case."

"Tink," Hank began again, purposely keeping his voice soft and gentle, not wanting to offend her with his next question. "Think about your wedding night. Could—could you, as his wife, give yourself wholly to him?"

She began to weep. "Th–that's the reason I haven't s–said yes to L–Lucky. I–I don't th–think I c–could."

For some unknown reason, a comment he'd heard on the evening news years ago popped into Hank's mind. When the newscaster had chided Wayne Gretzky, the well-known ice hockey player, in an after-game interview, for missing so many shots with the puck, he'd reminded the man, "You'll always miss 100 percent of the shots you don't take."

This may be my only shot, Hank told himself as he mustered up his courage, *and I'm going to take it!* He bent and kissed Tina on her cheek, then whispered in her ear, "Could you give yourself wholly to me, if the two of us were married?"

nine

Tina felt her body go rigid. What did Hank ask? Had she misunderstood his words?

"Well, could you?"

Through her tears she forced a smile. "Wh–what kind of a qu–question is that?"

"Just curious," he said, looking as if he wished he'd never asked it.

She relaxed and smiled to herself through her tears as Hank blushed. "You in the marrying market, Mr. Gordon? I thought you said you were afraid of falling in love again."

He gave her a sheepish grin as he brushed away her tears with the pad of his thumb. "I'm not afraid of falling in love, Tink. It's the landing that scares me!"

"I know. I guess in some ways I'm like that too, although I've never felt true love for someone like you have. It's the idea of committing yourself to one person for the rest of your life that terrifies me. I always told myself when I stood at that altar and said I do, I would mean it. I would make those vows with the intent of staying with that one person until death do us part."

"But you're willing to commit to Lucky!"

"I said, I felt I owed him my life, but I still haven't said yes to his marriage proposal. I just can't bring myself to do it. Not yet. But I can't put that decision off indefinitely. Bringing Gram back here and remodeling her house has just delayed it." Tina leaned her head onto his shoulder with a heavy sigh. "I just wish I loved Lucky like—"

"Like?"

In her heart she wanted to say *you*, but instead she said, "Like a wife should."

❧

Hank nuzzled his chin in her hair. *Oh, dear God, why? Why did you let Tink back into my life? I didn't need this. Not after losing my precious Sheila and then Glorianna. There for awhile I thought You'd sent Tink as the answer to my prayers. You know how I've longed to have a wife to share my life. She and I were getting along so well, having so much fun together, working side by side on her grandmother's house. Then Lucky appeared out of nowhere, staking his claims on her, taking her away from me, and I'm losing her, just like the others.*

"Hank?"

He pulled his thoughts together quickly. "Yes?"

"Tell me what it's like to be in love. Really in love, like you were with Sheila."

Hank sniffed at the sweet fragrance of Tina's hair. "Well, it's hard to describe that kind of love to someone else. At first you find yourself wanting to be around that person every minute." *Like I've wanted to be around you.* "You want to do nice things for them." *Like helping you work on your grandmother's house.* "You go out of your way to make sure they're content and happy." *Like I do when I worry about you and try to make sure things are going okay in your life.* "You find yourself thinking about them every moment you're apart." *I can't get my work done at the office for thinking about you.* "You try to provide for any needs they·may have." *I've wanted you to stay in my home rather than a boring old motel room, and I certainly wanted to make sure you ate proper meals and got a good, restful night's sleep!*

She nudged him in the ribs with her elbow. "Your description sounds like a mom with a new baby, not the kind of love I'm talking about," she told him in a teasing manner. "I'm talking about a love between a man and a woman."

Hank reassessed his words, amused at her reaction. "Umm, I guess in many ways, the love of a mother for her newborn child is much the same. She'd lay down her life for that child." He flinched and wished he hadn't uttered those words.

That was exactly what Lucky had done for her! "I–I mean—" he stammered, wishing he could withdraw his statement and begin afresh. "I–I mean, she's given birth to that child, and in some ways, it's still a part of her own body." *That made a lot of sense, Stupid!* he told himself angrily. "She—ah—"

"Lucky did that for me," she interjected quietly.

Hank wiped his hand across his eyes. *You big oaf, you're only making his case stronger. Think before you speak!* "Yes, I know he did," he said, being careful not to add more brownie points to his adversary's score. "But it's not the same. Oh, not that those things aren't valid, they are. But there's more to it than laying down your life for that person. Soldiers do it for people they've never even met when they take up arms and go to the battlefield. Firemen do it. Policemen do it too. Sometimes living with that person is the hard part. You know, once you're married, things change. Dating and saying I do are two different things."

"Different? How?"

"Well, all the time Sheila and I were dating, she looked like the perfect woman. I mean, her makeup was perfect, every hair was in place, she was always dressed beautifully. She said the right things, did the right things." Hank smiled and let out a chuckle. "And anytime I was with her, I made sure I was clean shaven, wore my best clothes, kept my hair cut like she liked it, took her to places she liked, even though I'd rather have gone someplace else. But—" He snickered.

"But what?" she asked, gazing up into his eyes.

"Well," he continued after adjusting his position a bit, "the honeymoon was perfect. We made over each other like we were a couple of lovesick teenagers. But once we got back to Juneau, things changed. For both of us."

"Changed? How?"

He grinned. "I'll never forget that first night after we got home. I was too tired to shower, so I just pulled out the old T-shirt I normally slept in and crawled into bed as soon as Sheila disappeared into the bathroom. Then ten minutes later she came out, looking like an escapee from a horror movie, with some weird-looking blue thing tied around her head and thick pink cream slathered all over her face. All I could see were two round holes where her eyes had been. I nearly screamed out in fright!"

Tina laughed. "Sure you did."

"Well, actually I wasn't scared, but I was sure shocked. This was not the woman I'd dated. Instead of that pretty pink nightgown she'd worn on our honeymoon, she was wearing a long-sleeved flannel thing that hung clear to the floor. I took one look at her and wondered if I was going to have to face this same monster each night of our life."

"Well," Tina said, nudging him again, "from the sounds of it, you didn't look much better. An old T-shirt? Come on. And I'll bet you didn't even shave before you went to bed. That after-five shadow of yours probably wasn't too appealing to her either. Did you shave on your honeymoon every night?"

Hank nodded slightly, hating to admit the truth. "Yeah, I did."

"Okay, go on. What else changed?"

"Lots of things. I was a struggling attorney at the time, just out of law school, and we really had to budget. I complained to Sheila constantly about her spending. I remember one time I even hit the roof because she'd bought drapes for our little apartment without asking me. We had a doozy of an argument and didn't speak to each other for days."

"I'll bet she had her complaints too. I doubt you were Mr. Perfect."

"Oh, yeah, and she let me know about them. 'Hank, don't leave your dirty socks on the floor. Hank, put the lid down on the toilet. Hank, wipe your feet before you come in the house. Hank, you play the radio too loud. Hank, don't use so much salt.' On and on and on. But I deserved all of it. I'd lived alone too long, I guess. I didn't realize those things were important to her. Just like she didn't realize how important my dog was to me. Or why I spent so much time tinkering with our old car. Or why I turned out the lights every time I left a room, or how leaving the lid off the toothpaste just didn't seem important to me. And neither did the tiny spots I left on the mirror when I used dental floss. That's all part of being married, Tink. I know each of these are only little things, but they're reality. Two lives trying to mesh together. They're the bits and pieces that take the bloom off the rose. Divorces occur because of the little things that get on people's nerves, their personal idiosyncrasies. I know. As an attorney I'm confronted with it every day as I try to help people weed out their assets after a divorce. Problem is, like it says in God's Word, we can't see the beam in our own eye. We never see our own problems. Only the other person's."

He waited, but Tina didn't respond. She just looked as though she was pondering his words, and he hoped he was getting through to her.

"It's even difficult for a couple to have an ideal marriage when they both love God, but it sure helps. A marriage happens, and suddenly you have someone else in your life to consider, and it's not easy, even if you love them. Especially if you've been living alone for a long time."

She eyed him suspiciously. "If marriage is so bad, would you ever want to do it again?"

"We're not talking about me, Tink." He shifted uncomfortably, not ready to answer her question, a question he'd deliberated on many times since having her back in his life. "And besides, I didn't say marriage was bad. I merely said things are different when you're dating than when you're married. It's not all fun and games. It's monthly bills, responsibilities, putting up with one another's faults and weird little habits—that sort of mundane stuff."

"What if another woman came along and swept you off your feet? Would you be willing to have another try at it?"

She'd put him on the spot and asked the one question he wouldn't even attempt to answer. He loved having Tina back in his life, and he wished he didn't have to constantly compete with Lucky for her attention, but marriage? As much as he thought he wanted another woman to share his life, was he actually ready to take another walk down the aisle to the altar? To take another chance on losing a woman he loved? "I'm—I'm not exactly sure," he finally said.

Tina eyed him for a moment, as if she wasn't sure what to say next, then stood to her feet, yawned, and, stretching out first one arm and then the other, said, "I'm beat. Let's call it a night."

Later, long after the house was silent, Hank knelt beside his bed, folding his hands in prayer and searching his heart before his heavenly Father. *God, I think I love Tink, but at this point in my life, I'm not sure what love really is. I did a lousy job of explaining it to her.* Remembering their conversation brought a smile to his lips. *I enjoy being with Tink, hearing her laughter, sharing her sorrows about her grandmother, helping her at the house, having her sit by my side in church on Sunday mornings—but—is it because I love her? Or because I've been alone so long and she's the first woman who has paid any real attention to me since I lost Glorianna? Could it be only friendship I'm feeling for her? Or is it the real thing? I've always heard loneliness does strange things to people. Am I reacting out of loneliness? Is this the reason Tina so willingly let Lucky into her life?*

He took a deep breath, letting it out slowly. *Oh, Lord, I don't know what I feel, but I sure don't want to make any more mistakes. Keep me from making a fool out of myself. Help me, please. Give me wisdom and discernment. When it comes to women, I'm at a total loss.*

❧

Early the next morning, long before Hank's alarm clock was set to go off, Lucky loudly wheeled the missing truck into Hank's driveway, hitting the trash can with a loud bang. Hank, Tina, and Faynola all came running from their bedrooms, wrapping their robes about themselves and hurrying to the door.

"You'd better stay in your room, Faynola. This could get ugly."

The woman nodded and scurried away.

Hank flung the door open just as Lucky reached for the knob.

"Well, howdy, folks," he said with a toothy grin, swinging the set of keys on his finger as if nothing had ever happened. "Breakfast ready?"

Tina rushed up to him and banged into his chest with her fists, her face red with anger. "How dare you show up here and even think of breakfast after what you've done, stealing from Hank, taking his truck like that, and disappearing?"

Hank's fists doubled at his sides, not because he was ready to strike out at the man, but because he was trying to control his anger. "If it weren't for Tina begging me not to call the sheriff, you'd be in jail right now," he snarled at the arrogant man.

"Aw, I wasn't worried. I knew she'd talk you out of it." Lucky flung one of his arms about Tina and pulled her close as she struggled to keep her distance. "My little Sugar Babe loves me. She'd never let you call the sheriff, would you, Honey?"

It was all Hank could do to keep from wringing the man's neck and holding him until the sheriff could come and arrest him. "My truck better be in one piece," he said in a low monotone, forcing himself to hold back his wrath.

With a snort followed by a belly laugh, Lucky let loose his grasp on Tina. "Your truck was okay 'til I hit that trash can someone left sittin' in the driveway."

"Give me the keys," Tina demanded, holding out her hand and standing toe to toe with the man, her eyes filled with rage. "Now."

Lucky's face sobered. "Ah, Tina, Honey, don't be so testy. I was just havin' me some fun, out meetin' some of these Alaskan Eskimos. I'm tired of workin' all the time."

This time Hank had to bite his tongue, hard, to keep from reminding Lucky who had actually done all the work on the house and who had quit his job.

ⅈ

"I should've called the sheriff myself," she told Lucky as he held the keys just out of her reach, her patience with the man at a final end.

"Aw, Babe. I was just teasin' you. I was really out lookin' for another job. I'd never—"

"Lucky, don't lie to me! You didn't quit those other jobs because you couldn't do the work! You got fired! Hank told me!"

Lucky whirled around and faced Hank with fire in his eyes. "He's the one who lied!"

Hank met his hard stare with one of his own as he pulled his cell phone from his belt and poised a finger over the keypad. "Shall we call one of your ex-bosses? Let him tell Tina why he fired you?"

"Are you calling me a liar?"

Tina cringed at the word, suddenly aware life was repeating itself. Her father had been a liar and a cheat, claiming others did him wrong, never able to hold a job, or even wanting to. How many times had they gone without food because he wouldn't get out and provide for his family instead of lying on the couch all day, guzzling his beer? Her parents' marriage had been a rotten one. Both her mom and dad had been miserable. When they weren't drunk, they were fighting or passed out on the couch. Did she want the same kind of marriage? Is that what life would be like married to Lucky?

"I'm the one who called you a liar," she shouted back at him. "Leave Hank out of this!"

"Leave him out of it? He's the one who's turned you against me!"

"If anyone turned me against you, it's you yourself! Not Hank!" she shot back, her heart racing with anger at herself for how foolish she'd been. For the first time since that fateful night when he'd come to her rescue, she was seeing the real Lucky. How could she have been so blind? He had been using her! Just like Hank had said.

Lucky whirled around and jerked his shirt up, exposing his bare back. "See that, Tina! That's what I got when I took those guys on for you. I nearly died savin' you! And this is the thanks I get for it?" He swung around and, with his thumbs pushing the waistband of his jeans down a couple inches, revealed a second scar, this one causing a deep indentation on his belly. "Old Hank ever put his life in danger for you like I did?" he shouted, leaning toward her.

"I would, if necessary!" Hank responded, without hesitation.

Lucky tugged his jeans back into place and gave Hank a mocking sneer. "Don't believe him, Tina, he's lying! He wouldn't do it."

Tina turned her head away, the sight of the deep scars bringing back the horrible remembrances of the night she'd worked hard to forget.

Hank grabbed a manila envelope from the drawer and pulled out a handful of official-looking papers, holding them out to Lucky. "Oh? And I suppose the Chicago police department is lying too."

Tina jerked the papers from Hank's hands and shuffled through them. "What are these?"

"Just a few police reports on some of Lucky's shenanigans. I got them from a friend of mine in the Chicago D.A.'s office."

"Lies, nothing but lies," Lucky shouted back in his defense, but the look on his face said otherwise, as arrogance turned to fear. "They're all against me. I never did none of that stuff."

Tina's jaw dropped as she read aloud from the first paper. "You have a police record?"

ten

When Lucky didn't answer she read on. "And you've been in prison? For armed robbery?" Her heart pounded against her chest as she thought of all the times she'd been alone with the deceitful man.

"I was framed," he said simply, with a sideways glance toward Hank. "The witnesses lied. Somebody paid them off."

Tina dropped down into a chair with a gasp as she flipped through the handful of papers. "You've been married! You told me you've always been single, and you've—"

"Three times!" Hank interjected, stepping up close to Tina, "and he's still married to his last wife."

Tina sucked in a deep breath and let it out slowly, shaking her head sadly and feeling like the most gullible person on the planet. "Oh, Lucky, I trusted you. You should never have lied to me like you did. And to think I was ready to marry you and spend the rest of my life trying to make it up to you for what you did for me."

"Keep reading, Tink," Hank prodded in a firm voice.

Tina blinked back the tears filling her eyes. She'd believed everything Lucky had ever told her, and he'd done nothing but lie to her.

"He's been arrested for domestic violence too. Several times. He beat one of his wives so badly she ended up in the hospital and had to have emergency surgery!" Hank said, pointing to the paper. "If you'd married him, his next victim could've been you."

Suddenly Tina's anger turned toward Hank. "You've known this and you didn't tell me?"

"The fax came in late last night," he explained quickly. "You were already in bed. I was going to tell you first thing this morning, but then that man came roaring into the driveway, waking us all up, and I didn't get a chance. I'd never keep something this serious from you, Tink. Surely you know that."

"He's jealous. He's always been out to get me, Babe. Come on back to Chicago with me. Let's get outta this screwy place. You and me don't belong here."

"You can't be serious! After what I've just learned about you, you think I'd go with you? Marry you?"

Lucky spun around, his eyes menacing and dangerous, the lines deeply set in his forehead, his fists clenched. After rambling off a bunch of obscenities at Hank, he added, "You're the cause of this. Me and her was doin' fine, until you came along. I oughta—"

Hank stood up to his full height, looking as if he was ready to do battle. "I'd think twice before swinging those fists of yours," he said coolly. "Remember, I'm the guy who is going to file charges on you for the theft of the money you took from my desk and stealing my pickup. Add that to the other things you're wanted for, plus leaving the state of Illinois without permission when you're still on parole—"

Tina's hand flew to her mouth. "You're on parole?"

"He sure is. And he's wanted for questioning on a burglary that happened the day before he left Chicago to come to Juneau." Hank walked quickly to the phone and picked up the receiver. "I'd say once I call the sheriff and let them know where you are, they'll come after you with lights flashing and sirens screaming, and you'll be heading back to prison."

Without warning, Lucky sprinted forward and grabbed Hank's shirt, pushing him into the wall, his nose mere inches from Hank's face. "I'm gonna get you, Mr. Lawyer. You and Tina! High and mighty people like you make me sick. If it weren't for you bein' so nosy and lookin' for any excuse you could find to take her away from me, nobody would've known I was in Juneau. Now because of you I'm on the run again." He jabbed an elbow hard into Hank's ribs.

"No, you're not going to blame me for this," Hank said

resolutely, his voice showing no sign of fear, his hand still clutching the phone. "You did this to yourself."

"I don't get mad, Hank Old Boy, I get even!" Lucky said through gritted teeth, as his elbow made another quick jab into Hank's ribs. "You'd better watch your backside! Both of you!"

Tina propelled herself into the man, one hand flailing at him furiously, the other still holding onto the papers. "Leave Hank alone! He's only trying to protect me!"

Lucky released his grip on his adversary's shirt and grabbed Tina's wrist. "I put my life on the line for you, and this is the thanks I get?"

Hank reached toward Lucky, but Tina waved him off. This was between Lucky and herself. It was up to her to get things settled.

"I do owe you, Lucky," she said, gulping hard. "If it weren't for you fighting those men off that night—" Her voice quavered a bit, but she went on. "When I saw how badly you were hurt, I vowed I'd spend the rest of my life making it up to you." Her emotions were about to get the better of her, but she hung on. "I would have. Even though I didn't love you, I was planning on marrying you. And—"

"Until he came along," Lucky shot in between her words. He grabbed the papers from her hand, wadded them up, threw them on the floor at her feet, then pointed a long bony finger toward Hank. "This rich lawyer made you forget all about old Lucky and the beating he took to save you from being raped—or worse!"

She cast a quick glance at Hank. "Being with Hank only made me see what real love could be. I'd never experienced that before. Can't you see, Lucky? Even if I'd married you, the truth about your prison record would have come out eventually, not to mention the fact that you are on parole and wanted for questioning and still have a wife! What kind of a life would that have been for either of us?"

Lucky's hold on her wrist increased, and she wanted to scream out in pain.

"You're no better than he is," he snapped, with squinted eyes and flaring nostrils. "I risked my life and what did you give me in return? The boot, that's what! When you ran into your old boyfriend! Suddenly what old Lucky had done wasn't so important to you!"

"No, that's not it at all," Tina countered. "You're a criminal, a liar, and a cheat, and still married!"

"Yeah? Well, that's the way I see it! To me, you and old Hank here are two of a kind, and I'm gonna—"

Hank stepped in between the two, squarely facing up to Lucky. "Yeah? And exactly what are you gonna do?"

"Like I said, I don't get mad, Hank Old Boy, I get even. I swear I will. I'm not going to spend another day in prison." Lucky stepped back a couple of steps, pulled a knife from his pocket, and released the long, shiny blade with a loud snap. "You file a complaint on me, and I'll kill you." He waved the knife menacingly through the air, its tip nearly touching Tina's chin. "Both of you!"

The malicious man turned on his heels and raced out the front door, leaving the pair gaping after him.

Hank threw his arms about Tina and pulled her close, his hand stroking her back protectively as the sound of his pickup starting and the squealing of tires told them Lucky had, once again, taken his truck.

"Now what?" Tina asked as she rested her head against him, her heart tensing with fear against his strong chest. "Do you think he meant wh–what he said?"

Hank placed a gentle kiss on her forehead before releasing her and grabbing the phone. "I'm sure of it. I'm going to call the sheriff."

She watched as he dialed the number, knowing it had to be done, despite Lucky's threat. Lucky was a menace to society. He'd been involved in armed robbery, and he'd served time in prison. It was only a matter of time before he was found.

❧

Hank watched Tina as he spoke to the sheriff. He couldn't

even begin to imagine the turmoil she must be experiencing at that moment, and he almost felt guilty for putting her through it. He'd had his suspicions about the man from the first moment they'd met. Tina had looked at Lucky through rose-colored glasses, seeing only his good points and his willingness to help her when she'd needed it.

When he finished his conversation, he placed the phone back in its cradle and turned to her, his expression somber. "Pack your bags. We're going away for a few days."

She looked up at him with the round, confused eyes of a child. "Why? Where are we going, and what about Gram?"

"She'll be safe. It's not her he's after. You can phone her and tell her where you are." The last thing he wanted to do was frighten her even further, but she had to know. "Did you read the last page of that fax I gave you? About Lucky? The notes my friend at the D.A.'s office added?"

She shook her head. "I didn't have time."

"He said Lucky was considered armed and dangerous and a real threat to society. That all precaution should be taken by anyone around him, especially those trying to arrest him."

Tina scrubbed a hand across her face. "Oh, Hank. What did I get you into?"

"You didn't get me into anything. I knew Lucky was trouble the minute I met him. I could've walked away then, but I didn't. I got myself into this with my eyes wide open. Don't blame yourself."

"I—I wish I'd been that perceptive."

He took her hand in his and lifted it to his lips. "You only saw in him what he wanted you to see. It wasn't your fault. Any woman in your shoes would have felt the same obligation." He smiled at her, hoping to somehow relieve her fear. "Hey, if he'd done that for me, I would have felt the same way."

"But he's threatened you. Both of us! I'm so afraid—"

"That's the very reason we're getting out of here for a few days, to give them time to find him. He can't get far. They'll get him soon, then we can come back home."

"But what if he talks one of the seaplane pilots into taking him to Anchorage or Vancouver or some other place? Like you thought he might have done before?"

What she was saying was, indeed, a possibility, one he hadn't wanted to voice. "Let's let the sheriff worry about it. They know what to do. I'm going to take you where he won't find us, just to be on the safe side. Although I doubt his threats to kill us were real," he said, trying to sound as if he believed it.

"But what if they were—"

Hank put a finger to her lips. "Go pack. We'll take Faynola and Ryan with us. I have a place where we'll be safe."

Thirty minutes later, the SUV backed out of the driveway with Hank at the wheel, Tina by his side, Faynola in the seat behind them, and the big Siberian husky in the back, with his nose pressed up against the rear glass.

❧

Tina caught a glimpse of Hank's strong face in the rearview mirror. How thankful she was for him. If she hadn't run into him in the department store that day, her life might have turned out very differently. She shuddered at the thought. What if she'd married Lucky, only to find out later he was still married? And had served time in prison? Had been arrested for domestic violence? And was even on parole? The thoughts made her stomach clench, and she thought she was going to be sick. But seeing Hank seated beside her, knowing he was doing all he could to protect her, set her mind at ease.

"Where are we going?" she asked, as they finally turned off the highway and onto a narrow winding road, covered over with a dense growth of trees.

"A friend of mine has a cabin up here." Hank gave her a wink. "Lucky won't be able to find us. We'll be safe."

She leaned her head against the headrest, linked her fingers together over her chest, and closed her eyes. "Good. I don't want to see you get hurt."

Hank let out a chuckle. "Me, get hurt? You don't think I can take care of myself? And you?"

She winced. "Not if Lucky has a gun."

He reached an open palm to her, and she slipped a hand into it. "Don't you realize, Tink, I wasn't kidding when I said I, too, would give my life to protect you?"

The words hit her right in the heart. Hank meant what he said! He would give his life to protect her.

"Did you hear me?" he prodded softly when she didn't make a comment. "That's what true love is all about, Tink. Loving the other person so much, their life is more valuable to you than your own. It's the kind of love between a man and a woman God speaks about in His Word. Not the kind of love Lucky said he had for you. His kind demanded retribution."

Tina pondered what he said. "But—you don't love me like—"

Hank gave her hand a squeeze. "Yeah? Who said?"

"What about groceries?" Faynola called out from the back-seat, unknowingly interrupting their conversation.

Hank let loose of Tina's hand and turned slightly in the seat to face her. "All taken care of. While you two were packing, I called the caretaker, and by the time we arrive he should have everything we'll need all stocked up. He and his wife promised to have the furnace turned up and a roaring fire in the fireplace."

❧

"Whose cabin is this?" Tina asked, as the two of them lingered over Faynola's coffee the next morning at the little table in the crude kitchen.

"Belongs to one of my clients. He's always after me to use it. I thought this was the appropriate time. Most folks don't even know it's here."

"The perfect place for hiding out?" Her lips curled into a slight smile. "Just what we need."

"Or a place to relax for a few days," Hank countered, taking on a smile of his own. "How about a hike in the woods? Pretty country out there."

Tina nodded. Her insecurities of yesterday seemed to have

faded somewhat with the good night's sleep. "Sure. I'd love it."

The two pulled on their heavy coats and boots and started up a path someone had made through the trees. It was a beautiful cloudless day, a perfect Alaskan day, the kind written about in travel brochures, picturing a late season snow.

"Why, Hank?" Tina asked him thirty minutes later as they came to a slight clearing.

Hank brushed the freshly fallen snow off the seat with his palm, sat down, and motioned her to sit beside him. "Why, what?"

"Why would you do all of this for me? I'm sure you have much too much work piled up in your office to take time off to watch over me."

He brushed a lock of hair from her forehead, then took her hand in his, his gloved thumb working gently over her knuckles. "Because you and your safety are important to me."

"But you haven't seen me since we were teenagers. It's been years."

He scooted a bit closer to her. "Don't laugh, but I've been asking myself the same thing. There's just something about you that brings out the hero in me, I guess. I like the feeling."

"I'm not worth it," Tina confessed, as she pulled her collar up about her neck. "You shouldn't be putting yourself in jeopardy to protect me. I'm a nobody."

"Of course you're worth it. Whatever makes you say such a thing?"

Tina sat silently for a moment. "You're so—so godly."

"Godly? Me?" Hank sat up straight. "I'm far from godly, although I'd like to be."

"Don't tease me, Hank. You know what I mean. Everything you do is right. Has meaning. You're—perfect."

"Oh, Tink, I'm far from perfect, believe me. You don't know what goes on in my head."

"Like what?"

Hank looked pensive. "Like the anger I felt the day Lucky kicked Ryan. Or when I found out he'd stolen that money from my desk. Or the way I wanted to punch his lights out when he treated you like he did. Oh, I'm far from perfect!"

"But—" She paused. "Wasn't all that what they call justifiable anger?"

He grinned. "Now you sound like a lawyer."

"Well, wasn't it?"

"Umm, I guess you could say so, but that doesn't make it right. I should've let God take care of it, instead of wanting to handle things my own way."

"See, that's what I mean. You're godly!"

He gave her hand a squeeze. "Tina, being godly isn't being a good person. Being godly means living by God's standards, with Him at the helm of your life. As Master of all you do, think, and be. Does that make sense?"

She gave him a slight nod. "Sorta. I remember hearing things like that when you and I attended Sunday school and church when we were kids. But that's been so long ago, I've forgotten most of what I learned. I hadn't been to church in years, until I came back to Juneau and started attending with you. Gram tried to talk to me many times about God, but I wouldn't listen. I—I thought she was being old-fashioned."

"It's never too late in God's sight."

"I'm not worthy of His love. I've turned my back on Him for so long. He's probably forgotten all about the little girl who used to pray to Him every night."

"He never forgets, and He's always waiting with open arms. A relationship with us is what He longs for most, but we have to invite Him into our lives. He won't barge in uninvited. And we have to confess our need of Him." Hank released her hand and slipped an arm about her shoulders. "As I recall, a skinny little girl with long pigtails went to the altar the same night I did and asked God to take charge of her life. Do you remember that?"

She leaned her head onto his shoulder. "Yes, I remember, and I meant it then, but—"

"Just tell Him you're sorry, Tink. Don't you know in Isaiah

49 He says He has engraved you on the palms of His hands? He's never forgotten you. Ask Him to move in and take up residence in your heart again. Put Him first in your life."

Watery eyes lifted to his. "And everything will be rosy?"

Hank laughed. "No, not rosy, but you'll have Him to turn to when things aren't rosy. He's always there to listen. His will, although at times we wonder about it, is always best for us."

She thought long and hard about his words. In her heart, she knew he was right, but was she ready to take such a step and commit her life to God? At this moment, He seemed so far away. "Let me think about it," she told Hank as she rose and pulled him up with her. "I'm not quite ready."

❧

Hank felt his heart clench. Tink had been so close to saying yes to God. He could feel it. If only he had the right words to make her understand. If only he was as godly as she thought he was. *Lord,* he prayed as he walked along close beside her, his heart filled with both sympathy and love. *If this is the woman You would have me spend the rest of my life with, now that Lucky is out of the picture, give me a sign. Somehow, let me know. I don't want to make any mistakes, for Tink's sake as well as mine.*

He'd barely gotten the words out of his mouth when a large tree fell across their path and a frightened Tina literally leaped into his arms. Hank smiled to himself. *Was that You, God?*

eleven

"I don't know when I've enjoyed myself this much," Tina confessed as Hank squatted down in front of her, with Ryan at his side, and snapped the clasp on her cross-country ski boots. "I'd nearly forgotten how much I loved Alaska."

"Kinda gets in your blood, living here. I've traveled to most of the touristy spots of the world, but there's no place like Alaska. I don't think I could live anywhere else." He snapped the other clasp and pointed to one of the mountaintops barely peaking over the trees. "I love this country. Have you ever seen a more beautiful place?"

Tina shielded her eyes from the morning sun and watched as an eagle soared high above them. "No, I wish I'd never left."

"You had good reason." He stood and stretched his arms wide, taking in a deep breath of the morning air. "I don't know how you stood living with your parents as long as you did."

"Maybe I should never have left them. Maybe if I'd stayed—"

"Tink, you did all you could. You have no reason to feel guilty."

She knotted her scarf tighter about her neck. "But maybe if I'd been more patient with him, Dad wouldn't have—"

"It was his choice, Tink. You could've been an angelic child, and he still would have taken his own life. If not then, sometime."

She stood silently as the eagle landed on the very tip of a tall tree, wondering at the magnificence of the mighty bird.

Hank couldn't keep his gaze off Tina. The rosy glow on her cheeks, brought on by the chilly Alaskan air, made her all the more beautiful. "Hard to tell. People drink for all sorts of reasons, but none of them make any sense. I guess they do it to avoid the realities of life."

"I don't think they ever loved me. Not really." She lowered her eyes. "I hate to admit it, but I was ashamed of them. When we had programs at school, I actually hoped they wouldn't show up, so the other kids wouldn't know I had drunks for parents. Wasn't that terrible of me?"

"No, I understand. I was there, remember? I saw the empty beer cans and wine bottles piled up on your front porch. Not to mention the dozens of liquor bottles and cans strewn about the yard. Living in that situation would embarrass any kid. I know you did what you could to make that place look presentable. You literally raised yourself, Tink. If their brains weren't fried, they'd have been very proud of you."

"That's no excuse. I should've been there for them. Maybe I was the problem. Maybe they never wanted kids. Maybe it'd have been better for everyone if I'd never been born."

He grabbed her arm. "Don't say such a thing. Of course they wanted you."

"We don't know that. They never told me they loved me, not once, and never treated me like your parents treated you!"

Hank had no answer. He knew firsthand what Tina was saying was the truth. He'd seen her father hit her for no reason at all. He'd seen her mother so drunk she couldn't even hold a hairbrush to Tina's head. He remembered the wrinkled clothes she'd worn to school because her mother wouldn't iron them for her. "My mom sure loved you."

She smiled. "Yes, I know. If it weren't for her and the way she took me under her wing and for my grandmother, well—I wouldn't have had any idea what a real loving mother should be like. I loved your mother too, and I'll always be grateful to her for being kind to a little ragamuffin like me."

"You were the daughter she wanted and never had. God only allowed them to have one child. Me!" Hank told her with a laugh as he pointed to his chest with his forefinger.

"You? Get serious, Hank. You were the delight of both your father and mother. You have no idea how lucky you were to be born to them. When I have children, I—" She stopped midsentence. "Maybe God won't let me have children. I know I'd be a lousy mother."

Hank slipped his arm about her shoulders. "Of course He will. He knows your heart, Tink. He knows what you've gone through."

"Do you think I was so hungry for love, I mistook Lucky's attention for the real thing?"

He had to examine his own motives before answering. "Maybe."

Tina pulled away from him and snatched up her ski poles. "Enough of this kind of talk. Let's get going!"

Hank watched as she took off across the clearing, and his heart went out to her. *Is what I feel for you sympathy or love?* Then lifting his eyes heavenward, he sent up a prayer. *Please, God. Send me another sign. Like I said, I sure don't want to make any mistakes.*

Supper was ready and on the table when the two came in from their day in the snow, and Faynola met them at the door. "You two are sunburned! Didn't you wear that sunscreen I found in the cupboard?"

Hank pulled off his stocking cap, then his coat. "Oops, I forgot. It's still in my pocket."

"You had sunscreen in your pocket?" Tina asked, hanging her coat on the hook next to his. "Why didn't you tell me? I would've used it. My nose is a bit sore already."

Hank touched the tip of her nose with his finger. "Because I think you look cute all pink like that."

"You'd better look in a mirror, Hank Gordon. You look like a raccoon with those big circles around your eyes!"

Faynola shook her head. "Will you two quit your bantering and come to the table? Things are getting cold."

After supper, Tina helped her clear the table and wash up the dishes before slipping into her nightgown, robe, and slippers. Hank had already had his shower and was sitting on the floor in front of the fireplace when she joined him. "Did you call your grandmother again?"

"Yes, she said she was fine and sends her love. I didn't give her many details. No sense in worrying her."

"It's been a good day, hasn't it?" he asked as she snuggled up close to him.

She nodded and leaned her head on his shoulder. "Umm, it's been a wonderful day."

"What'll we do tomorrow?"

She appeared thoughtful. "If we have to stay here tomorrow, how about building a snowman?"

He smiled and rested his head against hers. "I think there's an old fisherman's hat in the closet we can put on him, and I saw an old broom in the shed when I got the ski poles out."

"Maybe Faynola will let me have a carrot for his nose."

"We can put my muffler around his neck."

"You two sound like a couple of little kids," Faynola told them as she entered the room, her presence causing them to suddenly pull apart. "I'm going on to bed, but first I wanted to ask you, Mr. Gordon: Have you heard anything from the sheriff?"

Hank's boyish expression disappeared. "I'm glad my friend leaves his phone connected. I called the sheriff again, right after we got in tonight. Looks like we're going to be here for at least another day. They haven't found any trace of him, but—" He paused with a quick look toward Tina.

"What, Hank? Tell me."

"Someone robbed a convenience store about midnight last night, and the description the clerk gave them fits Lucky to a tee. Even the surveillance camera shot looked like him, even though the man had a stocking cap pulled down low on his forehead. Though I doubt he's out of money."

Tina let out her breath slowly. "Oh, Hank, no."

"Anyway, so far, other than him meeting their description, there's no sign of him. No one actually saw the vehicle he was in. He must've parked it out back. My guess is he stole another truck. They're still checking. But they're pretty sure Lucky was the guy on the videotape."

Tina swallowed hard. "And I'm the one who brought him

into all your lives."

"You can't feel that way, Miss Tina. It's not your fault," Faynola assured her, patting her arm. "No one blames you."

"She's right, Tink. You're not to blame at all. You only tried to help Lucky. You had no idea things would turn out like this."

Faynola yawned. "Well, good night. I'm going to go to my room and read. Let me know if you need anything."

Hank smiled at Tina. "We'll be fine, Faynola." When the pleasant woman was out of earshot, he added, "I love that woman, but three's a crowd."

She rested her head on his shoulder, and they sat staring into the fire, simply enjoying one another's company. It seemed to Hank nothing needed to be said. Just being together like that was enough. When the clock chimed ten, they said good night and went to their rooms.

As Hank knelt by his bed and folded his hands, he pursed his lips and shook his head. "I should've kissed her!"

He phoned his office early the next morning and discovered there were some important papers he needed to sign for one of his most prestigious clients. "I hate to leave you two by yourselves, but I think it'd be safer if I drove into town alone. What I have to do at the office will only take about fifteen minutes, and I'll head right back. You have the phone. If you need anything you can call the caretaker, but I doubt it'll be necessary. There's no way Lucky could know where we are, and I think his threats were nothing more than blowing smoke. He only wanted to frighten us."

"Oh, Hank, do you have to go?" Tina asked as she followed him to the door.

"Yep, but I'll be back quick as a wink. You'll hardly know I'm gone. I'm leaving Ryan here. Keep him in the cabin with you."

&

As promised, Hank was back in only a couple of hours, bearing two large shopping bags. One for Tina and one for Faynola. "You have to open them at the same time," he told them with a sly grin.

The two women giggled as each watched the other and, at the exact same time, pulled open the tops of their bags.

"Mr. Gordon!" Faynola shrieked as she pulled out a soft, fuzzy teddy bear dressed in overalls, with a big red bandana tied about his neck. "I love him." She hugged the bear tightly to her with a giggle. "I haven't had a teddy bear since I was six. Thank you so much!"

Tina took her time taking out her gift, although her hand had gone into the bag at the same time as Faynola's hand had reached into hers. "I like to prolong my surprises," she told Hank as she continued to feel around in the bag. "It's not a teddy bear, I can tell by his ears. It's not a duck, I can tell by his feet—"

"Open the bag!" Hank told her with an expectant boyish grin.

She ripped open the bag and pulled out another fuzzy stuffed animal. "A raccoon!" she squealed with delight. "And he looks just like you!"

"I figured you'd say that." Hank's face mirrored his joy at her reaction to the unexpected gift. "Do you like it? I stopped the SUV at the truck stop for gas, and they had these silly little stuffed animals. I couldn't resist getting them for you girls, being you're stuck up here at the cabin. I thought they might cheer you up."

"Oh, thank you, Mr. Gordon," Faynola said, still hugging the bear close to her. "I'm going to put him on my bed right now."

Tina waited until the woman was out of sight, then walked over to Hank and put her arms about his neck. "You old softie. That was so sweet of you. I'll keep him always. In fact, I'm going to name him Peter Pan, after the sweetest boy I've ever known."

The last words Hank had uttered before he'd gone to bed came to his remembrance. *I should've kissed her.* He wrapped his arms about her and pulled her close. Then taking his time, he planted a kiss in her hair, then on her cheek, on her nose, and then his kisses trailed slowly to her mouth. At first, barely touching her lips, then, rubbing his lips softly against hers until he could take it no longer, he kissed her like he'd longed to kiss her since that first day in the department store.

When their lips finally parted, he felt Tina melt into his arms as he held her tightly against his chest, never wanting this moment to end. "Oh, Tink. Tink. Tink. Do you know how long I've wanted to do that?"

She gazed dreamily up into his eyes. "Do what?"

He reared back slightly with a frown. "Kiss you like that!"

"Like what?" she asked, with big innocent eyes that tore at his heart strings and made him want to claim her as his own.

"You don't remember?" he asked, nuzzling his cheek against hers.

She smiled up at him with a mischievous smile that made his heart do a flip. "No, I don't remember. I guess you'll have to do it again."

Hank swallowed hard. "Happy to oblige."

"I thought we were going to build a snowman," Tina said softly as he pressed his lips against hers.

"Later."

It was nearly three by the time the two began gathering the snow into a mound for their snowman. They giggled and teased each other, occasionally tossing an ill-aimed snowball at one another. The sound of their laughter echoed in the hills around them, even bringing Faynola, with Ryan at her side, to the window to wave at them every now and then.

"Bet you can't find me," Tink told Hank as she shoved a handful of snow down his collar and took off on a run. "Close your eyes and count to fifteen before you come after me!"

He counted out loud, then took off through the trees after her. He tried to follow her tracks, but the fresh snow had fallen in mounds, making it difficult to tell which were tracks and which were the unusual formations caused by the snow falling from the tree branches. "Tink!" he called out loudly, once he'd decided perhaps he'd gone the wrong way. "Where are you?"

But no one answered, and he began to worry. What if Lucky had found them? Found her?

"Tink!" he called even louder. "This isn't funny! Where are you?"

Still no answer. He listened carefully, but there wasn't a sound, not even a rustling of the wind in the trees.

"Tink!" he yelled again, this time cupping his hands to his mouth. "Come out this instant! I mean it!"

"What a sore loser!" a lilting voice answered from somewhere behind him. "You barely gave me time to hide."

He turned quickly to find Tina perched on top of the shed, a mere fifteen feet from him. One hand went to his chest, while his other hand covered his mouth, his heart racing with relief.

"Help me down," she told him with a coy smile. "I won!"

Without a word, he went to the shed and lifted his arms to her. She slipped down into them easily.

"I was so scared," Hank admitted as he pulled her close and cradled her to him. "I thought Lucky had taken you from me."

Tina leaned into his strength. "Oh, Hank, I never meant to worry you. It was only a game. Like we played when we were kids."

"I know," he said, pulling her even tighter against him. "I thought I'd lost you. I won't leave you again until Lucky is caught and behind bars. I should never have driven into town to sign those papers. Nothing is more important to me than you. I—I—" He swallowed hard. Why was it so difficult to say it? "I—I—I love you."

Tina gasped. "You love me?" But she soon shook her head and pushed away. "Don't toy with me, Hank. Please."

Despite her protests, he pulled her close again. "I'm not toying with you. I—I know now—I do love you." He smiled as he remembered asking God for a second sign. "I only hope that someday you can love me too."

"I've loved you since we were four, Hank Gordon. There's never been anyone else. Not really. Aside from what I feel for you, the feelings I had for Lucky were the closest things I'd ever felt for a man. I'd tried to convince myself it was love, but all the time, deep down inside, I knew it was only gratitude. Not the kind of love I wanted. I was deluding myself. But what I'm feeling for you has to be that kind of love. You've asked nothing of me, even though you, too, said you were willing to die for me. I owe you nothing, but if necessary, I know I would lay down my life for you. I can't imagine anyone doing that unless they truly loved the person. That's why I was so confused about Lucky. I'm still not sure of his motives."

Hank's lips sought hers, and he found them cold from the chill of the Alaskan day, but filled with warmth and love for him, and he knew this was the woman God had sent to be his mate. But one thing remained a problem between them. Tina had still not given her life over to his Lord. Hank knew the two of them could not have sweet fellowship, as husband and wife, until she did. *Oh, God,* he called out from deep within his heart, desperately needing God's guidance. *You've given me two signs already. But would You plant this kind of love in my heart for a woman who doesn't love You? I need another sign. Just to be sure.*

"Hank?" she whispered against his kiss. "Tell me more about how God sent His Son to die for us."

Hank quickly sent up a thank-you prayer before spending the next hour with his Bible, going over God's plan of salvation with the woman he loved.

❧

"Supper's ready," Faynola called out to the two sitting on the sofa in front of a blazing fire.

Hank closed his Bible and took Tina's hand in his. "You have no idea how happy you've made me, by asking me to explain the Scriptures to you, Tink."

She smiled up at him as his arm encircled her waist, and they walked into the little kitchen. "I'm glad I've made things right with God. I never meant to separate myself from Him. It just happened."

"Made your favorite, Mr. Gordon," Faynola told him as she placed a big square of lasagna on his plate.

Hank's eyes lit up. "Don't ever let anyone steal you away from me, Faynola."

"No way, Mr. G. I like working for you. I was just telling Mr. Bojangles this afternoon what a kind, considerate man you are."

Hank frowned. "Who is Mr. Bojangles?"

"My teddy bear!" she answered, with a snicker. "The one you gave me!"

They all had a good laugh.

"I'm going to phone the sheriff again, right after supper," Hank told them, as Faynola placed another square of lasagna onto his plate. "I don't like the idea of that man being out there without us knowing where he is, and you need to get back to your grandmother."

Tina nodded. "Me either. I'm so afraid he'll try to make good on his threats, and I'm worried about Gram."

A sudden noise made them all jump.

"It's him!" Hank shouted, knocking his chair over as he leaped to his feet. "I recognize the sound of my truck. You ladies stay here! Keep Ryan with you. I'm going—"

But before he could get out of the room, the sound of shattering glass penetrated the house, causing them all to back away from the archway between the living room and the kitchen. Glass shards shot through the room like bullets, and a rock hit the wall opposite the glass panel by the front door.

"Get down!" Hank ordered as he shoved the women toward the kitchen table. "Under there, and don't come out until I tell you."

"But where—"

Hank gave Tina a look that told her there wasn't time to ask questions. "His quarrel is with me. Stay put!"

As Hank started into the living room, Lucky began pounding on the door, shouting obscenities, and using God's name in vain.

"Get out of here, Wheeler!" Hank shouted at him, as he hurriedly crossed the room, small pieces of glass crunching beneath his shoes. "No one wants you here, and we don't want any more trouble. Do yourself a favor and leave!"

"Don'tcha wan yur truck back?" Lucky yelled out, his words slurring.

Hank could tell by his voice he'd been drinking, which, he knew, made the man even more dangerous. "No, take it with you and go."

"You and me has a score to settle," Lucky yelled back, slurring his words even more.

"Not as far as I'm concerned. Now get out of here." Hank checked to make sure the door was locked, then leaned his back against it.

He waited for an answer, but Lucky didn't make another sound. *Where is he?* Hank asked himself. *And is he armed?* He shot a glance at the gun cabinet. He hadn't let Tina know, but he'd checked it that first night, after she'd gone to bed, making sure there was plenty of ammunition. In case he needed it to defend the three of them.

"Lucky?" he called out.

No answer.

He looked toward the kitchen door and could barely make out the two women crouched beneath the table, but was relieved to see them there, especially with Ryan at their side.

Had Lucky decided to go around to the back door? The one off the kitchen? Was it locked? He couldn't take a chance on leaving his position. So in as loud a voice as he dared, he called to Tina, telling her to make sure the door was locked. He watched as she moved out from under the table, his heart pounding with fear for her safety, until he saw her return and slip back down beside Faynola, whose eyes were as round and large as the saucers she'd used at their dinner table.

"Lucky," he called more loudly, once he was satisfied Tina was safely back under cover. "Answer me! What do you want?"

Still no answer.

Then he heard the truck start and the tires squeal, as Lucky backed out and turned into the narrow drive leading down to the main road. The man was gone.

"You can come out now," Hank called out to Tina and Faynola.

The two women warily joined him in the living room, Ryan at their side, both of them trembling and shaken from the experience.

"What did he want?" Tina asked as she melted into his open arms.

"He never said. I couldn't get him to answer. All he said was he had a score to settle with me. Those were his last words. And he was dead drunk. Men don't think straight when they've got alcohol under their belt. I don't like this at all."

"How did he find us?" Tina asked, clutching tightly to his arm.

"Must've seen me in town and followed me out here. I thought I was being careful. I circled around a bit before heading back to the cabin."

"Now what?" Faynola asked with a shaky voice as she hung onto Ryan's collar.

"Now he knows where we are. I think we'd better head back into town. Fast. I'm calling the sheriff. You ladies get whatever you need to take with you. We'll leave the rest here and come back for it later. I want to be out of here in no more than five minutes."

The women did as they were told, but when Hank picked up the phone there was no dial tone.

The phone was dead.

twelve

Hank stared into the receiver. *Lucky must've cut the phone line on the outside of the house! Too bad my cell phone won't work here in the mountains.* Not wanting to worry Tina and Faynola, he placed the phone back in the receiver and hurried to retrieve his briefcase and the few things he wanted to take with him before turning down the thermostat on the furnace and securing the screen in front of the smoldering fire. He hurried into the little attached garage and found an odd-shaped piece of plywood and a few nails and a hammer. The plywood wasn't perfect, but it was large enough to cover the narrow window panel Lucky had broken out.

"We're ready," the two women said, as they rushed breathlessly back into the little living room, each with a stuffed animal and a small bag in their hands.

Hank motioned them out, then pulled the door shut behind him, making sure it was locked before leading the way to the SUV. But when they reached the vehicle, the sight that greeted them made them all gasp. The windshield was shattered. Lucky had bashed it in with a big rock.

"Oh no," Hank said, as he moved closer for a better look. "He's slashed all four tires too!"

Tina dropped her bag and buried her face in her hands. "Oh, Hank. It's all because of me."

Faynola wrapped her arm about Tina. "Don't worry, Miss Tina. The sheriff is probably on his way right now. He'll take us back to town."

Hank bit at his lip. "I'm afraid the sheriff isn't coming. Lucky cut the phone line."

Now it was Fanola's turn to cry. It broke Hank's heart as he watched the two women huddled together, wrapped in each

145

other's arms, trying to comfort one another.

"We'd better get back in the cabin," he told them, trying to keep his voice from betraying his fear for their safety. Once they were inside, he sent them into the kitchen to put the coffee pot on. He used that task to keep them busy while he pulled several guns from the gun cabinet and loaded them with ammunition. For all he knew, Lucky could've parked the truck and walked back in. He might even be hiding behind a tree or the shed or in the dense foliage, watching them.

"Guns?" Tina asked him, as she came back into the room, carrying two cups of coffee, the cups chattering on their saucers as she carried them with unsteady hands that betrayed her fear.

"I'm sorry, Tink. I know you're afraid of guns, but I have no choice. I don't think Lucky would follow through with his threats, but you—" He stopped and let her finish the sentence for herself. He was sure by now she knew all too well what Lucky was capable of doing. He took a cup from her and forced a smile he hoped appeared confident. "Just a precaution, that's all."

"I–I—know."

After turning on the outside floodlights, he asked Faynola to stay in the kitchen and watch for any movement at the back of the house. Hank shoved the couch across the room and took up a position in front of one of the larger windows. He wanted to keep vigil and have a panoramic view of the front entrance and the road. Unless Lucky walked back in through the woods, he'd have to come this way.

Tina settled in close beside him, fear etched on her face. "If I'd known all those things about Lucky, I would never have gotten anywhere near him, no matter what he'd done for me."

Hank placed the rifle across his knees and slipped his arm about her shoulders. "I've been thinking about that. You know, Lucky had to have had some good in him to stop that night when he saw you were in trouble. Too bad the good part didn't win out over the bad."

"Do—do you think God could forgive someone like Lucky? After all he's done?"

Hank's arm tightened about her. "Of course He could, Tink. In fact, sometimes it's easier for a man to realize he's a sinner when he has a record like Lucky does, than when he's just an ordinary Joe going to work to support his family every day."

Tina smiled and rested her head on his shoulder. "Good. Maybe someday Lucky will get right with God, like I have."

The long, dark hours of the Alaskan night dragged on and on, with no sign of the frightful man. About midnight, Hank sent the women on to bed, promising to keep vigil. He knew it would be difficult for them to sleep, but with Lucky on the loose, no telling what might happen, and he wanted them to be rested. He also knew, although Tina had been concerned that he might fall asleep, there was no way sleep could overtake him as long as his Tina was in danger.

She joined him at the window at six the next morning, urging him to get some sleep while she kept watch. "Please, Hank. I'll awaken you if I see anything."

He'd barely gotten to sleep when she caught sight of a red pickup edging its way slowly up the road. With panic seizing her, she shook Hank. "A truck's coming, but it's not the same color as your truck! Do you think Lucky has stolen another one?"

❧

He jumped to attention, fully awake, and grabbed up the rifle. But his frown and the determined set of his jaw disappeared quickly as a smile broke across his unshaven face. "It's Trapper!"

"Trapper? Are you sure? Why would he be coming up here?"

"I'd know that truck anywhere!" Hank said as he stood the rifle against the wall and rushed toward the door. "I helped him put that rack on to hold his kayak."

By the time the truck came to a stop in the driveway, Hank had donned his coat and was out the front door. "Hey, am I glad to see you! What're you doing up here?"

"Got worried about you," Trapper answered, as he exited

the truck and the two men shook hands. "Your secretary called me late last night and said she'd been trying to reach you for hours, but the operator kept telling her the phone was out of order. I figured I'd run up here and check on you. Good thing you told me where you were going."

Tina rushed out of the house and threw her arms about Trapper's neck. "Oh, Trapper, God must've sent you!"

The man did a double take. "God sent me? What do you mean?"

"Come on in, and I'll tell you all about it," Hank told him as he took his friend's arm and ushered him toward the cabin. "Tink's right. God had to have sent you."

A little over an hour and a half later, after the four of them, along with Ryan, had wedged themselves into Trapper's truck, the little group arrived back in Juneau, safe and sound.

"We got him less than an hour ago," the sheriff told them as he met them in the outer office. "The guy's got nerve. One of my men spotted your pickup parked in back of your house. Would you believe the drunken idiot was actually asleep in your bed? Looked like he'd broken in through the kitchen. Pretty dumb, huh? Leaving the truck exposed like that."

Hank offered a slight grin. "Yeah, pretty dumb. But at least you caught him, and we can all go back to our lives, without having to worry about him and his threats. He probably figured he was safe, with the three of us stuck up there at the cabin without a phone."

"What'll happen to Lucky now?" Tina asked, holding tightly to Hank's hand.

"I'm not exactly sure yet. He'll have to answer to us for what he's done here in Juneau. Then I imagine they'll send someone from Chicago to pick him up and take him back there. Looks like he's going to be locked away for a long time."

Hank extended his right hand. "Thanks, Sheriff."

"Need a ride home?"

Hank shook his head. "No, thanks. I think Trapper'll take us."

Trapper smiled. "No problem. That's what friends are for."

Tina stood on tiptoe and kissed Trapper's cheek. "You have no idea how much I appreciate you checking on us like you did."

"Don't thank me. God made me come. He wouldn't let me sleep, just kept me thinking about you two, until I got out of bed and drove up there."

"God leads in strange ways sometimes," Hank said, remembering the three signs he was sure had come from God when he'd asked for them. "Let's go home."

❧

Tina grinned as Hank doused his pancake with maple syrup. "I'm going to go see Gram this morning and get her things all packed up, in preparation for her move. After that, I'm putting up the Christmas tree and decorating it. My next project will be to cook supper for you, Hank!"

Faynola placed another pancake on Tina's plate. "Oh? Taking over my job, are you?"

Tina's fingers grasped the woman's arm. "Oh no, Faynola. I could never do that. I couldn't compete with you."

The woman smiled down at her. "I'm glad you've come back into Mr. Gordon's life, Miss Tina. I've watched you two find each other. It's been more romantic than any romance novel I've ever read, and I've had a front row seat. You two belong together. I could've told you that the first week you came to stay here at the house."

"You should've told me," Tina said, with a childlike glance toward Hank. "It would've saved us all a lot of time and grief. I guess I'm a slow learner."

"You had reason to be," Hank told her with a wink at his housekeeper as he forked another bite. "Lucky had a pretty tight hold on you."

Tina smiled at both of them. "That's all over now. I'm free."

❧

"Isn't that the most beautiful tree you've ever seen?" Tina asked Hank after dinner, as they sat locked in each other's arms on the sofa, staring at the hundreds of tiny twinkling lights wrapped around the plump evergreen.

"Uh-huh," Hank answered in barely a whisper, turning to look at the lovely woman next to him. "But what I'm seeing is more beautiful than any old Christmas tree."

She swatted at him playfully. "Keep those words coming, Peter Pan. A girl can never hear too many compliments."

"I mean every one of them."

"Guess what else I got done today?"

He brought her fingers to his lips and kissed the tips of them, one at a time. "What?"

"I got my computer all set up and even made contact with my office. I was afraid they'd think I was never going to get back to work, but they assured me things have been a bit slow. I think they only said it to make me feel better. Anyway, I told them I was bringing Gram home and would be ready to get back to work, full-time, by Monday. I can't believe they've been as understanding as they have."

"I can. I'll bet you're a terrific employee."

She smiled appreciatively. "I try."

"I did something today too. I rented a hospital bed for your grandmother, from that medical supply house downtown. I'm sure she'll be more comfortable on it than on a regular bed."

Tina straightened. "But they're so expensive! I wanted to rent one for her, but—"

"My treat. Don't give it another thought. They're delivering it the first thing tomorrow. We'll call it one of her Christmas presents."

"Oh, Hank. Are you sure you're not my guardian angel, instead of a mere mortal man?"

"Quite sure," Hank told her with a mischievous grin, as he tilted her chin and stared into her eyes. "No angel could feel about you like I do. It's a privilege given only to us mortals."

❧

Early the next morning, the couple stood at Harriett Taylor's bedside at the nursing home, holding hands. "We're here to take you home, Gram," Tina told the frail woman. Her dream was finally coming true. She was taking Gram to the house on

Ocean View Boulevard, fulfilling her wish.

Her grandmother wept openly as she extended a delicate hand covered with huge brown spots. "I–I can't begin to t–tell you how much this m–means to me. You've m–made this old woman very happy."

"I know, Gram. That's why I wanted to do it." Tina took hold of the small hand and gave it a squeeze. "But I couldn't have done it without Hank. I can't tell you all he's done for me. And the work he's put in on your house!"

"Don't listen to her, Mrs. Taylor," Hank said modestly. "She's exaggerating. Besides, we've both loved every minute of getting your house ready." He gave the old woman a wink. "It gave me a good excuse to be around your granddaughter."

The woman leaned back into her pillow, her free hand going to her heart. "Praise God, I'm so glad Lucky is out of your life, Tina. As grateful as I was to that man for what he did for you that night, I never liked him. Or trusted him. He was not the man I'd asked God to give you." She cast a quick glance toward Hank. "But I have a feeling He's answering my prayers."

Tina felt Hank's hand on her shoulder. "He did, Gram. He sent Hank back into my life. Through him, and his patience with me, I've come back to God. I've given my life over to Him and accepted Christ as my Savior."

Mrs. Taylor closed her eyes. "Oh, you dear ones. I'm so happy. Now I can die in peace. God has answered my prayer, even above and beyond what I ever dreamed. I know Hank is a fine man. He'd have to be—he's a Gordon. He's proven that by the way he's taken care of you while you've been in Juneau. I was so relieved when you phoned and said you were staying at his house. I loved his parents." A tear rolled down her wrinkled cheek. "I–I—just wish my son would have been—"

Tina leaned over and pressed her face against the old woman's. "You did all you could, Gram. Dad and Mom were just not cut out to be parents. Their bottle of liquor was more important to them than I was. In one of his messages, our pastor here in Juneau said all a parent can do is try to raise a child the way God would have you raise them, but the final decision rests with them. You did your best. Daddy just chose to live differently than you'd taught him. So did Mom. They both knew better. They just didn't care."

"I'm so thankful Hank's parents were good to you. Heaven only knows what your life would've been like without their influence."

"Me too," Tina agreed as she stroked her grandmother's forehead. "Hank has arranged for an ambulance. We're here to take you home, Gram."

≥

The smile on Gram's face when Hank carried her into the little house on Ocean View Boulevard made every bit of their work worthwhile. "Welcome home, Gram," Tina said, pulling the old double wedding ring quilt over the frail body before bending down to kiss her grandmother's cheek.

Hank's heart filled with awe at Tina's dedication to the tiny, nearly helpless woman in the bed. He wished he could take away all the hurts Tina had suffered at the hands of both her parents and Lucky. Not much in her life had gone right, yet she'd managed to land a decent job, work hard, get promoted, and never forget her allegiance to the one person who'd loved her all those years. Harriett Taylor.

"Thank You, God," the slight woman said softly, as she folded her hands. "Thank You for hearing this old woman's prayers. I'm finally home." With that, she closed her eyes and fell fast asleep.

Tina placed a kiss on the tip of her finger, then transferred it to her grandmother, barely touching the wrinkled forehead, before smiling up at Hank, her eyes filled with grateful tears. "Yes, she's finally home, and just in time for Christmas. Thanks to you."

≥

"Good morning. Tina Taylor. How may I help you?"

Hank leaned back in his desk chair and smiled into the

phone. "Hey, what a cheery voice. You have a great phone presence."

"Hi, Hank."

"So? How's it feel to be back to work again?"

"Wonderful! I'd almost forgotten how it is to be an important, viable part of the Beesom Parts team. Not much happening at the main office because of the holiday, but I've been on the phone and the Internet most of the morning, getting back into the swing of things."

"How's Harriett doing?" he asked, doodling oddly shaped hearts on a scratch pad as he talked.

"Doing better than I was afraid she might after her first night home. I was afraid she'd be exhausted. But she had a good night's rest and ate a big breakfast. Now she's watching her soap operas on TV," she told him with a giggle. "She got hooked on them at the care home. She said that's all they did all day."

"Well, at least those soaps keep her busy so you can do your work. Faynola made up a big pot of venison stew, so you won't have to cook tonight. I know it's not a very fancy dinner for Christmas Eve, but I thought your grandmother might enjoy it. The two of us, and Ryan, will be there about six."

"I know Gram likes venison stew. She's told me many times how she used to make it for my grandfather. You're too good to me, Hank. I'm glad you're bringing Faynola and Ryan. I want Gram to meet them."

"Get used to me being good to you, Kiddo. This is just the beginning. See you around six."

ﾅ

By six o'clock, Tina had helped her grandmother bathe and dress in a fresh gown. She'd had her own shower, and the two of them were ready and waiting expectantly when Hank and Faynola arrived, laden down with the boxes of food Faynola had packed. He smiled at the two of them, as Ryan bounded in past him. "How are my favorite ladies?"

Harriett Taylor lifted her head from the pillow and reached

out a hand. "Hank. Dear, dear Hank. What a sweet man you are. Just seeing that handsome face of yours makes this old lady feel young again. And that beautiful dog must be Ryan. Tina told me all about him."

Hank put the boxes on a chair, moved quickly to the bed, and kissed her cheek. "Aw, careful there, you'll give me a big head."

Tina had already placed a card table next to the hospital bed, covered it with a bright red tablecloth, placed a colorful candle and candle ring on it, and set it for three with her grandmother's lovely white dishes and monogrammed silverware. Then she'd taken a red napkin and added the same white dishes and silverware to her grandmother's tray. After giving Ryan one of the venison bones to keep him busy while they had their meal, Faynola helped Tina put the rest of the things on the table, and the four enjoyed a hearty dinner.

Once things had been cleaned up and put away, Faynola pulled a chair close to the old woman's bed, and the two ladies prepared for a good visit, while Hank and Tina moved into the living room and Hank built a fire in the fireplace. Once the logs had taken hold and begun to burn, he lowered himself to the floor and wrapped his arms about Tina. For long minutes they sat there, warming themselves by the fire, staring at the bright lights of the Christmas tree. It seemed conversation was no longer necessary between them. Just being together was enough.

Tina nestled in close to him, loving the manly scent of his clothing, his hair, his aftershave. Lucky had never smelled pleasant like that. He'd always smelled of leather and the grease from his cycle. She wondered how she'd ever tolerated it. Just the thought of it now made her cringe.

"It's hard to believe Christmas is already here," Hank finally said. "I'm glad we're spending it together. Without Lucky."

Tina nodded dreamily. "Me too."

Finally, at ten, Faynola came into the room with Ryan trailing along beside her, telling them she'd gotten Harriett ready for bed and tucked in for the night, and the old woman was fast asleep. She busied herself tidying up the room and pulling her coat from the hall closet, giving the couple time to say their good nights in privacy.

Hank gave Tina one final kiss, then pulled himself away, motioning Ryan toward the door. "See you tomorrow morning."

🏵

Hank and Faynola arrived at nine Christmas morning with a partially cooked turkey and all the fixings for a grand meal.

He found Tina all showered, her hair curled up like he'd never seen it before, and she was wearing a pretty red dress. As she and Faynola went into the kitchen to finish preparing Christmas dinner, Hank went into Harriett's room to spend some time with her.

"Would you read my Bible to me?" she asked as she gestured to the big old family Bible Tina had placed on her bedside table. "I'd love to hear the Christmas story from the second chapter of Luke. These old eyes can't focus on the words any longer."

Hank nodded, opened the Bible, and with a smile began to read, taking note of all the comments Harriett had penned into the margins. Tina's parents might have been losers, but praise God, she had a concerned grandmother who loved God and had prayed for her all these years.

After a marvelous Christmas dinner, Hank carried Harriett into the living room and lovingly laid her on the sofa on top of the quilt Tina had spread out for her, placing a pillow beneath her head. The old woman's eyes filled with tears as she looked upon the colorfully lit Christmas tree, filled with the ornaments she'd collected over her many years. "This is the best Christmas ever," she told them, blinking hard. "I never thought I'd actually make it home again, but you two have made it happen, and I am so grateful."

"I have presents for my three best girls," Hank added, moving to the base of the tree and picking up three beautifully gift-wrapped packages. He handed a gift to each one with a flourish of his hand.

"You first," he told Harriett.

"But I didn't get you anything," she said sadly.

"Yes, you did. You gave me the best present I could ask for. Your granddaughter."

She gave him a quick smile as she pulled the ribbons from the box and opened it. Inside was a lovely pink bed jacket with matching pink slippers. "Thank you, Hank. They're perfect."

"You next," he told Faynola.

She grinned and pulled off the ribbons from her gift. "Oh, Hank, blue, my favorite color." She held up a snuggly soft chenille robe with matching slippers. "How did you know my size?"

"Easy. Peeked in your closet when you weren't looking." He turned to Tina. "Now you," he told her, holding out her gift.

"I can't," she told him, her heart touched with his generosity. "You've done so much for me already."

"Open it, Tink. Please."

She dabbed at her eyes with her sleeve and began to pull the ribbons and the paper from the small box. She let out a gasp as she pulled out a second box, a small velvet one, and lifted the lid. "Oh, Hank. A diamond watch! You shouldn't have. It's much too expensive!"

"Nothing is too expensive for you, Tink." He took the little box from her hand and removed the watch. "Here, let me put it on you."

She held out her arm. He opened the clasp, slipped the dainty watchband over her wrist, and pressed the catch until it closed with a snap. "Now you won't have to keep asking me what time it is."

"But you—"

He put a finger to her lips. "No more. I wanted you to have it. I just hope you like it."

Tina stared at the tiny gold face circled by a ring of diamonds. "It's the most beautiful watch I've ever seen. I'll cherish it always."

"It's not nearly as beautiful as the woman I bought it for."

She backed away quickly. "I have a present for you too. But it's nothing like the one you gave me. I'm almost embarrassed to give it to you."

"Whatever it is, it'll be special because it came from you."

She hurried to the closet and brought back a flat, rectangular box, wrapped in brown wrapping paper and tied with hemp twine. Attached to the twine were three hand-carved wooden stars and a tiny little card made from parchment paper, with *To my Peter Pan, with love, Tink* hand lettered in green ink. "It's not much, but I hope you'll like it," she said apologetically, as she placed it in his lap.

Hank read the little card, then fingered the beautifully hand-carved stars, turning them over and over in his hand. "Where did you get these? I've never seen anything like them."

She gave him a bashful look. "I–I carved them. With that old pocket knife I found at Gram's. I used to carve a little bit when I was a kid, when I'd hide in the woods behind our house to avoid my father's beatings. Sometimes, when I was especially frightened, I'd be there for hours. Carving helped to pass the time."

"I'll keep them always," Hank said, carefully removing the stars from the twine and slipping them into his shirt pocket. "Just because you made them for me." He pulled the twine from the package, then the paper. "Oh, Tink! This is wonderful! Who did it?" He held up a framed hand-sketched picture of his parents for Faynola and Harriett to see. "Did someone locally do this for you? It looks exactly like them!"

"I–I did it," she answered softly, hanging her head. "I sketched it from a photograph I found in that album in your living room bookcase. I know how much you loved them."

Hank's eyes widened. "You did this? I didn't know you were so talented. Tink, this is as good as any professional artist would've done! I'm amazed."

"You're just saying that to make me feel good."

He moved quickly to her side and pulled her into his arms

again, tilting her face up to his. "No, I'm saying it because I mean it! There isn't another gift you could have given me, at any price, that would have pleased me more. Oh, Tink, thank you. Merry Christmas, Sweetheart." He bent his head and tenderly kissed her lips. "Your grandmother is right! This is the best Christmas ever. And just the first of many, if I have my way about it."

Wrapping her arms about his neck, Tina returned his kiss. "Merry Christmas, you wonderful, thoughtful man."

Later that night, after placing the precious picture of his parents on his nightstand, Hank knelt by his bed and thanked the Lord for the many blessings He'd bestowed upon him, especially for sending Tina back to him. *And Lord, thank You most of all for speaking to her heart and making her see her need of, once again, having a relationship with You. You've answered my prayers, abundantly above what I asked.*

❧

New Year's Day passed by quickly, and so did the first two weeks of January. Each day, Tina and Hank watched as Harriett Taylor's strength waned. The doctor came to the house often to check on her, since she was much too weak to get out of bed. Each time, he warned Tina and Hank to be prepared for her passing. It could come at any time.

During the evening of January the twentieth, Harriett called Hank and Tina to her side. "Hank," she said in a voice so faint he had to kneel next to her just to hear her. "Please, would you pray for me? I'm ready now. I want to go home, to my heavenly home. Would you ask God to take me? I'm so tired, and the medicine no longer takes away the pain."

Hank nodded, and after kissing the old woman's cheek, he took both her hands in his and bowed his head. "God, You know how much Tink and I love Harriett and how hard it is for us to even think of losing her. But her heart and her body are giving out on her, Lord, and she's ready to—to come to You."

Tina watched as he swallowed hard and pressed his eyelids tightly together, knowing how difficult it must be for him, and loving him for doing what her grandmother had asked.

"We thank You that we were able to get her house ready in time to bring her home for Christmas," he went on, "and for the weeks we've had with her since then. But now she says she's ready to go to her heavenly home. She's—she's asked me to—" Slowly, he looked into Harriett Taylor's aged face, his tears flowing unashamedly. "I'm sorry. I can't say it. I just can't."

A feeble hand came to rest on his shoulder, as the woman motioned him near and spoke with great effort in a faint whisper. "It's okay. God knows what I asked you to do. Thank you, Hank, you're a good man."

Harriett slipped away quietly in the middle of the night, a smile on her face that only her Lord could have put there.

"I don't know what I'm going to do without her, Hank," Tina told him between sobs as she watched them take her grandmother away. "She was the only link I had to my past. The only living relative I knew about. Now I'm all alone."

"No, Tink, not alone. I'm here. I love you, and I'll never leave you. We need to be grateful for the time we've had with her."

Tina threw her arms about his waist and held on tight.

"At least your grandmother got her final wish. She died at home."

*

The funeral was held on the twenty-third at Hank's church. As Tina stood by him, singing the songs her grandmother had requested, she thought about all the pain the woman had gone through with her son, Tina's father. Her precious, sweet grandmother had suffered so much, yet she'd never turned away from her Lord. How was she ever going to get along without that saintly woman? The only blood relative who'd ever truly loved her?

"Harriett Taylor loved God," the minister was saying. "And she loved her granddaughter, Tina Taylor. Many of you knew Harriett when she lived in Juneau a number of years ago and are here because you've lost an old friend. Many of you didn't have the privilege of knowing her and are here because you've come to love Tina in the short time she's been with us here in this church. Harriett Taylor will be missed, but do not mourn as those mourn who have no hope. Harriett Taylor is in the arms of her Lord, as she'd asked. No more will she endure the pain inflicted on her by her mortal body. This is a day for rejoicing!"

Tina glanced around at the many people gathered in the church, her church family now. Trapper, Glorianna, their children, Faynola, and dozens of others. Just the sight of them made her heart glad. Although she would miss her grandmother and life would never be the same without her, she knew the minister was right. It was a day for rejoicing. Her grandmother was in heaven with her grandfather. She smiled up at Hank through tears of happiness and tightened her grip on his arm. "Thanks, Hank, for helping me fulfill my grandmother's dream. I could never have completed it in time without you."

His hand cupped hers. "No thanks needed, Tink. I did it because I wanted to. And I'm here to stay. You can count on it. Others might've failed you, but I'll never let you down, I promise."

She leaned into him. "Do you realize her last wish, to die at home, is what brought us together?"

"I sure do, and I'll always be grateful to her."

⁊⁊

Hank spent long days at his office, catching up on the things he'd left undone when he'd come to Tina's rescue. Evenings and weekends, the two were inseparable. Spending their time together in front of the fireplace, listening to CDs, reading from the Bible, and enjoying one another's company. Hank could barely wait to get to the house on Ocean View Boulevard at the end of the day.

"I rarely see you anymore," Faynola complained to him one evening in mid-February, as he rushed in to shower and change clothes before going to spend the evening with Tina.

Hank grinned. "You should be glad. You don't have to cook for me."

"I like cooking for you." She watched as he flitted around the room nervously. "What's the matter with you? Did you lose something?"

His smile broadened. "Nope, just have things on my mind."

❧

All through dinner, Tina kept her gaze on Hank. For some reason, tonight he wasn't himself. He seemed fidgety. Nervous. She wondered if he was having misgivings about what she thought was their budding relationship. She was happier than she'd ever been, but did Hank share her happiness? Maybe he wished he'd never gotten involved with her topsy-turvy life. But hadn't he promised her he was there to stay? Finally, she could stand it no longer and decided to confront him. "Is anything wrong? Have I done something to upset you?"

He shook his head and, with a mischievous grin, took her by the hand and led her to the sofa in front of the fireplace. He sat down and pulled her onto his lap. "Know what day this is?"

She gave him a coy grin. "February fourteenth?"

He nodded. "Valentine's Day."

She pulled away from him slightly, took a large white envelope from the top drawer of the end table, and handed it to him. "Happy Valentine's Day, Hank. You thought I forgot, didn't you?"

He opened the envelope and pulled out a valentine, showing two people sitting on a couch in front of a blazing fireplace, hugging each other. He gave her a wink and read the words aloud. " 'Some folks may like to go to Paris. Some might like to go to Rome. Some might like to visit the pyramids. Me? I'd rather be right here at home. With you! I love you, Peter Pan. Tinker Bell.' " He bent and kissed her cheek. "Thanks, Tink. I hope you mean those words."

"I do mean them," she said, tenderly stroking his cheek. "I love our times here in front of the fireplace. And I love you."

"Now you," he said, reaching under the toss pillow and pulling out a crumpled white envelope. It looked as if it had been run over by a Mack truck.

She frowned. Why would he give her something in such pitiful condition? She tried to appear not to notice and pulled open the flap. What she found inside made her heart sing with joy. It wasn't the lovely, lacy, expensive Valentine she'd expected to receive from Hank. It was a homemade one, created from red and white construction paper by a third-grader many years ago. Filled with excitement, she pulled it from the envelope and pressed it to her breast. "Oh, Hank, I love it. I thought you'd thrown it away."

"Read it," he told her, his face quirked into a smile.

With a song in her heart, she wiped the tears of joy from her eyes and read it aloud with great emotion. " 'Tink is pretty. Tink is smart. I'll love you forever. Here is my heart. Be my Valentine.' And it's signed, Peter Pan." She threw her arms about his neck and planted kisses all over his face. "Oh, Hank, I love you too!"

He pushed her away. Surprised, she stared up into his face, wondering if she'd misunderstood his card.

"Will you?" he asked, as he reached into his jacket pocket and pulled out a small white box tied with a red satin ribbon. "Be my Valentine? Every day of our lives and not just on Valentine's Day?"

Too filled with emotion to do anything but nod, she took the box from the man she loved and hurriedly untied the ribbon, hoping it contained what she thought it did, but fearing it didn't.

Hank's hand reached out and covered hers. "You have to answer me first. Will you?"

She leaned into him, the box still in her hand, half opened. "Of course I will! Oh, Hank, I love you so much it hurts. I think I always have. I can't even find words to express my love for you."

He gave her a satisfied grin. "Okay, then. Open your gift."

With trembling fingers, she yanked off the ribbon, then the

paper, and opened the little white velvet box inside. Her palm went to her mouth as she let out a loud gasp. "Oh, Hank, it's beautiful!"

He took the lovely pear-shaped diamond solitaire from the bed of velvet and slipped it onto her finger. "Will you marry me, Tink? Be my Valentine forever?"

"Oh yes. Forever and ever and ever and ever. I love you, Peter Pan!"

Hank swept her up in his arms. "We've wasted way too much time. I want us to get married as soon as possible."

"Me too. I want so much to be your wife."

He became serious. "Remember the question I asked you? About your wedding night, if you married Lucky?"

Tina well remembered his words. Those words were what caused her to question her loyalty to Lucky and made her see what her life would have been like if she'd married him. "You asked if I could wholly give myself to you if the two of us ever married. I'll never forget that question as long as I live. I nearly went into shock!"

"What's your answer, Tink?"

"Oh yes, my dearest. Yes, yes, yes! I can hardly wait. I know now loving you is going to be the sweetest experience of my life."

Hank brushed his lips across hers. "You mean the sweetest experience of our lives."

"The sweetest experience of our lives!" she said, correcting herself, then added with an excited giggle, "Would it be too soon if we set the wedding for three weeks from today?"

≥

The church was packed with friends and neighbors. The pastor was standing at the altar. The groom was there, and so was the best man. Everything was in readiness for the wedding of Hank Gordon and Tina Taylor, except for one thing.

The bride was missing.

thirteen

Hank stared at the closed double doors at the back of the chapel. *Where is Tink?* He glanced at his watch. The ceremony was to have started fifteen minutes ago. Was history repeating itself? Was he going to be left at the altar again?

"Don't worry, Hank," Trapper said, patting his shoulder reassuringly. "She probably got delayed in traffic."

Hank's brows lifted. "In Juneau? On a Saturday? Not likely."

"Maybe she had a flat tire. Maybe the—"

"Maybe she decided not to marry me after all!" Hank said with a slightly angry tinge to his voice. "Is this déjà vu?"

"No, and don't you even think it. That woman loves you."

Hank yanked the bow tie from his neck. "Yeah? Then where is she?"

Trapper clutched his friend's arm. "Give her a few more minutes."

"Do you think we should dismiss the audience?" the pastor prodded gently, as if not wanting to upset the already upset bridegroom even more. "It's beginning to look like she isn't going to make it. Surely she would've phoned the church by now if she'd had a problem getting here."

Hank lifted his hands in exasperation. "Yeah, send them home, or let them stay and eat the cake. I don't care. I'm leaving!" With that, he rushed down the aisle and out of the church. His face filled with anger, his heart ached with grief. He searched the parking lot for signs of her car and, finding none, headed the SUV for the house on Ocean View Boulevard. Seeing Tina's car still parked in the driveway, he pulled to a sudden stop behind hers and pulled out the house key she'd given him. He was determined to rush in, have it out with her, and ask for his ring back. He'd spent big bucks on that ring, and if she wasn't going to marry him, the least she could do was return it.

But the house was empty.

When he called out her name, she didn't answer. He checked each room. Her wedding gown was hanging in her bedroom, her veil lay neatly spread out across the bed, her hose and satin slippers lay on the chest. He pulled open the closet doors, expecting to find her clothing gone, but everything was in its place. Where was Tink? Why hadn't she gotten dressed and come to the church as planned? If she'd planned to leave and not go through with the wedding, why hadn't she at least left a note? None of it made any sense.

With a heavy heart, filled with both disappointment and rage, he drove the SUV across town to his home. Faynola met him at the door. "That friend of yours in Chicago just called. I think he said he was a district attorney. He wants you to call him immediately! He said it's urgent! I tried to call you on your cell phone, but you must've turned it off."

"Did he say what he wanted?" Hank asked as he quickly looked up the number and dialed the phone.

"No, but from the sound of his voice, it must be something important!"

The man answered on the first ring. "Hank! Man, am I glad to hear your voice. We've got trouble here. I just learned that guy you asked me about, that Lucky Wheeler? They were transferring him to another prison, and the van got hit by a bus. Some of the passengers were injured, and in the confusion, he walked away. He's been on the loose for four days now, and so far they don't have a clue as to his whereabouts. I thought you should know, in case he tries to come back to Alaska, which is doubtful. We think he's still in the Chicago area."

Hank went numb. Lucky escaped? Could that have anything to do with Tina's disappearance? Frantic, he phoned the sheriff.

"I'll get out another APB right away," the man told him.

"You don't think he'd come all the way from Chicago to Alaska again, do you?"

"I hope not, but you never know. He made some pretty serious threats, and Tina didn't show up for our wedding today. I'm worried."

"Oh, Hank. I'm sorry. Do you have any idea where she might be?"

He lowered himself onto the desk chair. "No, I just hope—"

"Let us know if we can do anything to help. Maybe it was only wedding jitters. I hear that happens to brides once in awhile. They just take off without telling anyone, to think things over."

Hank thanked the man, then leaned his head against the wall. He had no idea where to begin to search for Tina. He wasn't even sure he wanted to, not if she'd deliberately left him standing at the altar, the laughingstock of all their friends. Yet what if she was in danger? What if Lucky had come back to Juneau? He dropped to his knees by the chair and pled with God to help him find his Tink. He had to at least know she was safe.

Each time the phone rang, Hank darted to answer it, but each time, it was well-meaning friends asking about Tina. He checked with the sheriff one last time about two in the morning and finally fell asleep on the sofa, exhausted, the phone by his side.

When it rang at four A.M. he grabbed it up quickly, expecting to hear the sheriff's voice, but the voice on the other end was definitely not the sheriff's. He could barely hear what the person was saying and nearly hung up, thinking it was a prank call.

"Who is this? Speak up," he told the caller angrily, resenting being awakened at that hour for nothing.

"Hank, it's me—me. Tina," a faint voice said. "Lucky c–came to the house and f–forced me to go w–with him."

Hank clutched the phone tightly. He could tell she was crying. "Where are you?"

"At y–your friend's c–cabin."

Thank God my friend had the phone line repaired. "Why, Tink? Why did he take you there? Did he say?"

"To keep me from marrying you. He wanted to ruin our wedding. He—he said it was to get e–even with us."

"Has he hurt you?"

"No, he hasn't hurt me, b–but he's been drinking h–heavily. I'm so a–afraid of him. I'm afraid he might—"

"Where is he now?"

"H–he finally passed out. He's a–asleep on the couch, but he has the k–keys to the old car he's d–driving in his pocket. I c–can't get to them, and I'm a–afraid to start walking. I–I don't know what to do. He—he has a gun."

Hank jumped to his feet and began pacing back and forth, as far as the phone cord would allow, running his fingers through his hair nervously. *God, what do I tell her? I'm nearly an hour away from her.*

"Hank, I'm s–sorry about our wedding," she said softly into the phone, and he could tell she was still crying. "You kn–know I'd—"

He stopped pacing. "Listen to me, and do exactly what I say," he told her, hoping his plan would work. "Can you see the gun?"

"Yes, it's lying on the s–sofa beside him. But I'm a–afraid of g–guns, and I could never sh–shoot anyone!"

"I know, Sweetie. Walk carefully over to the sofa, pick up that gun, then open the outside kitchen door and leave it standing wide open."

"Y–you want me to leave the c–cabin?"

"No, you'd freeze out there. But if Lucky wakes up and sees the door open, he'll think you've left and go after you."

"Then wh–what shall I do?"

"Take the gun with you, go into that upstairs closet, and cover yourself with blankets, pillows, anything you can find. He probably won't even think to look for you in the cabin. Don't come out for any reason until I get there. Do you understand?"

"Yes," she said, faintly between sobs. "I'll o–open the back door, then take the g–gun upstairs with me and h–hide in the closet until you get here. But h–hurry, Hank. I'm scared."

"Pray, Sweetheart. You're not alone. God is with you." He pressed the phone tightly to his ear, not wanting to miss one word. "Tink."

"Yes?"

"If he should come upstairs and find you, you know you might have to shoot him, don't you? To defend yourself."

"I could never sh–shoot anyone!"

"We'll pray it won't come to that, but Lucky is a desperate man, and he's drunk. He's liable to do anything. I just want you to be prepared. I'm coming for you, my love."

"Oh, Hank. H–hurry, please hurry!"

"I'm on my way."

Hank phoned the sheriff, then leaped into the SUV and drove at breakneck speeds, pressing the accelerator to the floor. He had to get to Tink before Lucky woke up. "God, please protect her," he cried out as his hands gripped the steering wheel. "I'm sorry I ever doubted her. I should've known better. Please, God, please comfort her, and keep her safe until I get there!"

It seemed to take forever before he reached the narrow road leading up to the cabin.

❧

Tina lay covered beneath a pile of blankets and pillows on the floor of the closet, holding her breath and praying. *God, please! I've turned my life over to You, and I'm trusting You to keep me safe until Hank gets here. Don't let Lucky find me, I beg you! And keep Hank safe. Lucky hates him and would like nothing better than to harm him.* She held her breath and lay motionless, her heart pounding so loudly she was afraid Lucky might hear it.

His drunken voice suddenly boomed out angrily, echoing through the cabin. "Tina! Where are you? You can't hide from me!"

Fear gripped her heart. *What if he comes up those stairs and finds me?* She listened, hoping he'd discover the open kitchen door and go in search of her as Hank had said he would.

"Oh, so you've taken out on foot, have ya?" she heard Lucky yell out, then the slamming of a door, and she breathed a bit easier. Hopefully, he'd taken the bait. *I've got to do exactly as Hank told me and not come out until he comes for me. Lucky may still be down there.*

❧

As the SUV approached the house, Hank could see several marked cars in the driveway and breathed a sigh of relief. The sheriff and some other officers had arrived ahead of him, just as he'd hoped. He leaped out of his vehicle and hurried toward the three officers standing by one of the cars.

"We got him," the sheriff called out. "The idiot was wandering around in the trees. He was so drunk he could hardly stand up. He didn't even put up a fight."

"Where's Tina?" Hank asked frantically, not even glancing at the man secured in the back of the sheriff's car. She was his only concern.

"Don't know, Hank," he said, sadly shaking his head. "We've asked him, but all he would say was she left while he was asleep. He was pretty upset because he couldn't find her. I've got two men searching the woods for her now. Wish I could tell you more."

Hank smiled. "I think I know where she is." With that, he darted up the steps of the cabin, taking them two at a time, and bolted through the door, calling out her name.

❧

Tina pushed back the blankets, quilts, and pillows at the sound of his voice and rushed from the closet, throwing herself into his arms as they met at the head of the stairs. Praise God! Her Hank had come, and she was safe!

The feelings of love she felt as she pressed herself against him overwhelmed her. "Oh, Hank, I missed our wedding," she said sadly. "Can you ever forgive me?"

Hank brushed aside a tear and held her close. "Oh, Tink, if anyone needs to ask forgiveness, it's me. When you didn't show up at the church, I thought you'd decided not to marry me after all, and I was furious!"

Her hand rose to stroke his cheek. "Never, my love. I'd never leave you like that. I love you too much to hurt you."

"And I love you, Tink." He buried his face in her hair. "I prayed for God to protect you, and He did. We have much to be thankful for."

She snuggled her face against his broad chest, drinking in his masculine fragrance. "I prayed he'd protect you! I was afraid you'd confront Lucky. He was so drunk, and he might have had another gun in that old car—"

"Shh!" He put his fingers to her lips. "Everything's okay now. The sheriff is probably already on his way back to town, with Lucky locked in the backseat. He won't bother us again. They'll make sure he's locked up tight this time."

"And we can get married? As we'd planned?"

Hank pulled her close. "Oh yes, my precious, as soon as possible! Only this time, you're not getting out of my sight on our wedding day."

A grin formed on her tear-stained face. "Don't you know it's bad luck for the groom to see the bride on their wedding day?"

Hank threw back his head and let loose with a loud belly laugh. "Bad luck, Tink? I don't think any piece of bad luck could be worse than what we've gone through already!"

fourteen

"Well, Old Buddy," Trapper whispered in Hank's ear as they stood at the front of the church a second time, waiting for the music to begin. "Here we are again."

Hank fingered his bow tie. "Yeah, I sure hope things go right this time. My batting average is at rock bottom when it comes to weddings."

Trapper rested his hand on his friend's shoulder. "Don't worry. Glorianna's with her. She won't let her get away this time."

Hank let out a big sigh. "I sure hope you're right. I couldn't stand being left at the altar again."

❧

"You look beautiful," Glorianna told Tina as she straightened her veil for her. "I can hardly wait to see the look on Hank's face when you walk down that aisle toward him."

Tina turned to smile at the woman she'd come to love almost as much as a sister. "I really love him, Glorianna. I just hope I can make him as happy as you've made Trapper."

"Don't worry, you will. You two were made for each other. I love Hank like a brother, but he and I were never destined to be together. It was always Trapper I loved. I think, deep down, Hank and I both knew that from the beginning."

Tina slipped her arm about Glorianna's shoulders. "I realize that now, but at first I hated you for what you two had done to Hank. Now I realize you and Trapper did the best thing for everyone, and I love you both for having the courage to do it." The two women embraced, but separated quickly as the music sounded.

"Are you ready?" Glorianna asked, her face aglow with happiness for her new friend. "It's time to start down that aisle. I've had strict orders from both Hank and Trapper to make sure you didn't get away."

Tina took one step toward the door, then panicked, her hands going to her throat. "My necklace? Where is it?"

Glorianna gasped. "I don't think you were wearing a necklace when you got here."

"I don't remember putting it on," Tina said, nearly in tears as she fingered her bare neck. "Are you sure I wasn't wearing it?"

"Pretty sure. Could it be in your bag?"

Tina turned quickly, eyeing the small bag she'd brought with her. "I don't think so. At least, I don't remember putting it in there. Oh, where is it? My brain has been so scattered all day!"

"Hold on, I'll check." Glorianna carefully stepped over the long satin train and grabbed up the bag, quickly searching its contents. "It's not in here!"

"What am I going to do? My beautiful heart-shaped necklace. I have to wear it!" Tina blinked hard and dabbed at her eyes.

"Be careful. You're going to mess up your makeup." Glorianna pulled a tissue from the box on the vanity and handed it to her. "You're the bride. Everyone will be looking at you, not me. You can wear my necklace."

"You don't understand! Hank bought that necklace for me to wear at our wedding! He made such a big deal of it! He said if we ever had a daughter, she'd be able to wear it at her wedding. He wanted it to become a family heirloom, and I've lost it! He'll be so disappointed if I'm not wearing it!"

Glorianna put a consoling hand on Tina's arm. "Take it from me, Sweetie, as beautiful as you look in that gown, he'll never even notice."

"I hope you're right." Tina dabbed at her eyes, again, trying to calm down. She'd just have to explain to Hank later that she'd misplaced the necklace. Surely he'd understand.

"The organist has already played the bridal song once. We'd better get out there, or Hank and Trapper will come looking for us."

Tina nodded. "I'm ready, I guess."

Glorianna knelt to pick up the train again, and as she did, she let out a second gasp. "There's a velvet box on the floor under the table!"

"That's it! That's my necklace!"

&

"Where is she?" Hank turned to Trapper as the bridal song ended, and the organist played the introduction for the second time.

Trapper shrugged. "Got me!"

Hank tugged at his cummerbund, his eyes pinned on the double doors. "Think she's changed her mind?" he asked in a half whisper.

"Be patient, Old Man. Maybe she got her veil caught in her zipper or a run in her stocking. Who knows about women? As long as I've been married to Glori, I still don't know what makes her tick."

Hank bit at his lip. *Come on, Tink. Don't disappoint me again! Not a second time!*

Finally, the double doors parted and Glorianna appeared, donned in a pink silk organza gown and carrying pink carnations. When she reached the front of the church, Tina appeared in the open doorway, in a long flowing bridal gown of white satin and beaded silk organza, and she was wearing the diamond heart-shaped necklace Hank had given her.

Hank caught his breath. He couldn't take his eyes off his bride as she moved slowly toward him. She was a vision of loveliness. Her smile told Hank everything was going to be fine this time. *Surely no man has ever loved a woman more than I love Tink.* He wanted to run down the aisle, sweep her up in his arms, and carry her to the altar, but he restrained himself and waited.

"Down, Boy," Trapper said over his shoulder with a snicker.

Hank laughed nervously, then licked at his dry lips. *Hurry, Tink, hurry! I've waited so long for this minute.*

When she joined him at the altar, he couldn't resist and

slipped an arm about her waist, pulling her close to him, kissing her lips right on top of her veil. "I love you, Tinker Bell."

She smiled up into his face. "I love you too, Peter Pan."

The pastor cleared his throat loudly, and the audience laughed. "Are you two ready to get on with the vows, or shall I just pronounce you husband and wife and get it over with?"

Hank looked up at him with a broad grin. "No, Sir, let's do this up right. I've got an arm around her now, and she can't get away. Take as long as you like."

A Letter To Our Readers

Dear Reader:

In order that we might better contribute to your reading enjoyment, we would appreciate your taking a few minutes to respond to the following questions. We welcome your comments and read each form and letter we receive. When completed, please return to the following:

Fiction Editor
Heartsong Presents
PO Box 719
Uhrichsville, Ohio 44683

1. Did you enjoy reading *Be My Valentine* by Joyce Livingston?
   ❏ Very much! I would like to see more books by this author!
   ❏ Moderately. I would have enjoyed it more if

   _____

   _____

   _____

2. Are you a member of **Heartsong Presents**? ❏ Yes ❏ No
   If no, where did you purchase this book? _____

   _____

3. How would you rate, on a scale from 1 (poor) to 5 (superior), the cover design? _____

4. On a scale from 1 (poor) to 10 (superior), please rate the following elements.

_____ Heroine	_____ Plot
_____ Hero	_____ Inspirational theme
_____ Setting	_____ Secondary characters

6. How has this book inspired your life?_____

_____

_____

7. What settings would you like to see covered in future
   Heartsong Presents books? _____

_____

_____

8. What are some inspirational themes you would like to see
   treated in future books? _____

_____

_____

9. Would you be interested in reading other **Heartsong
   Presents** titles? ❏ Yes   ❏ No

10. Please check your age range:
   ❏ Under 18   ❏ 18-24
   ❏ 25-34   ❏ 35-45
   ❏ 46-55   ❏ Over 55

Name_____

Occupation _____

Address _____

City_____ State_____ Zip_____

E-mail_____